Eros Unmasked

Dirk Mourningwood

DYINGSTAR PRESS LLC

Dyingstar Press LLC

Dave,

I hope you reap what this sows.

Introduction

You've come to the third installment of Eros, bringing the sum to twenty-four spicy stories. The first offering, Eros Unzipped, began with a note— a warning?— that the stories derived from past experience. Since that starting point, the stories have taken on their own life. Characters have returned and taken on their own life. I've attempted to capture some viable situations, but others are just ridiculous. I'll leave it to you to decide which is which.

Trigger warnings — feel almost unnecessary to include in a book of eight male-on-male erotica stories. Prepare yourself for graphic drug use, sexual acts, and strong language. The sex isn't always safe; those involved aren't always sober. There are age gaps and power dynamics, but no one is forced.

Also By Dirk

Other works by Dirk Mourningwood
La Luce's Legacy (2024)
Eros Unzipped (2024)
Eros Unchained (2024)
Eros Unmasked (2025)

Contents

Art Class

As an amateur photographer, my ex was obsessed with me finding my own creative outlet. I told him my spare time was mine to spend as I wanted, and if I wanted to spend it playing video games or reading, that was my choice. He was insistent, pushing and pushing me. After all, his photography had been pivotal to our getting together. Our first meeting turned into our first date, with five hundred pictures of me and three of him.

Four months after Jorge moved out, I finally relented. I signed up for the community center's Adult Mixed Media Artist Expression class. I showed up with nothing, and the instructor— guide? teacher?— Mrs. Brown gave me an old set of charcoal pencils and a sketch pad with twenty pages left in it. I had no idea what I was doing, but enjoyed it enough that I found myself looking up tutorial videos over the next week.

On the fourth week, the center of the room, which normally had a vase of flowers or complex sculpture to ignite our inspiration, now only had an empty, plain wood chair. The other students filed in, setting up their oils or watercolors. One was a sculptor with a block of clay. As was my norm, I hadn't introduced myself to any of them, but we exchanged friendly nods and smiles while we set up.

"Welcome, welcome," Mrs. Brown trilled as she entered the room with her flowery overcoat flowing behind her like a wave. "I have a special treat for everyone. In the next two weeks, we will have a single focus point. As always, work on a single piece or individual details. Your time is yours to spend as you wish."

All eyes shifted to the movement at the door and the man entering wearing a plush white hotel robe. Soccer Mom beside me made a soft "Oh..." while straightening in her chair. The older man on my other side grunted, but I wasn't sure what he meant by it, nor did I care. I was too torn between deciding what to do. I'd either slink away through the back door before the model noticed and recognized me or I'd call out to my old roommate, the first guy I was ever with.

His dark eyes washed over the room, not pausing on me, as Mrs. Brown waved him to the center dais.

I apparently had chosen a third option, to stay but remain silent.

"Since the inception of art," Mrs. Brown said, "we have strived to capture the human form—masters and amateurs from every culture and creed. Our souls yern to understand and reproduce the curves that should be innately known to each of us. Omar will be our topic these next two sessions. Familiarize yourself with his form and allow the muse to flow through you." She waved to the chair. "Omar, if you are ready."

He shrugged off the robe, exposing his tan and perfect skin for the class. He sat in the chair, throwing a knee over an armrest so his legs were spread wide in my direction. His eyes flicked over me without a hint of recognition before settling into a pose with a hand behind his head, facing away from me.

Fucking hell. Raj Singh, or Omar as he was going by for this modeling gig. I thought about him often enough over the six years since we were roommates in college. I could have drawn his naked form from memory, with how much time we spent showing off for each other in our dorm or me jerking him off in the laundromat's supply room. He was bigger now, with his pecs popping and abs pronounced down to the V leading to his soft, uncut cock. His thighs and biceps were an order of magnitude bigger than I remember, too.

I don't know how long I stared at him— studying him, as Mrs. Brown might assume I was doing. My erection pressed painfully against my pants, and I risked my neighbors noticing for me to adjust myself.

Soccer Mom gleefully painted his abs, moving downward. I shot my load on the belly those abs were now chiseled out of more times than I could count. I'd taken his on mine just as often.

The old man's watercolor was fixated on how the light played against Raj's armpit hair. An armpit that I'd buried my nose in and ran my tongue up. His smell was always intoxicating; a blend of beard oil and lotion. Raj had more body hair than I remembered, but kept it neat and trimmed. His pubes... Fuck, I wanted to run a finger down that dick and cup those balls. He never reciprocated what I did to him in that storage room, but he never objected or stopped me.

How were we never caught going into the janitor's closet once, sometimes twice, a week? We were never that careful about cleaning up before we slipped out. Like one of the times Raj let me eat his ass in there. He was bent over, moaning and sweating, then completely painted a bottle of disinfectant on the metal shelf in front of him. I wiped it down with a wad of paper towel, but that couldn't have been enough. We were really fucking dumb.

Mrs. Brown was making her rounds, and my paper was blank. I scratched out the lines of Raj's jawline, keeping it rough to represent the stubble. He'd trimmed back the carefully manicured beard he kept before. I wasn't sure if I liked the new look.

"Excellent, Sophia. Your attention to shading is exceptional," Mrs. Brown said to Soccer Mom beside me, then was looking down over my shoulder. "Well, Marshal, it looks like you're enjoying yourself." That was her usual to me. It was never a compliment or critique of my work, just a comment that I must be having fun.

I used what remained of the ninety minutes staring at my old roommate while my cock tried to rip through my pants. I outlined his total pose, made a popup focusing on how his dick draped across his balls, and spent the last bit working on his profile and the distant, unfocused gaze in his dark eyes.

A bell chimed softly. Raj had the robe over his shoulders and was out the door before Mrs. Brown could say anything.

"Thank you, Omar," she said as the door closed behind him. "We will resume in a week. Consider if you would like a different angle, but he will adopt the same pose for continuity."

"We had a direct line, huh?" Soccer Mom whispered to me, and I chuckled and grinned back at her.

***

"He just stormed out? Fucking prick." Samantha finished her set at the fly machine and stood for me to take her place.

"Maybe he didn't recognize me?" I offered back.

"Bullshit, Marsh. He might have packed on thirty pounds of deliciousness, but you're the same. Are there any spots left in this class, by the way? I could bring my crayons."

"No, the session's full. What do I do? It about killed me to stare at him, looking as perfect as ever, only to be ignored like we'd never met."

"You could skip next week and let me go in your place."

"Please?"

Samantha huffed. "Force him to see you. Put yourself right in his line of sight so he has to see you; has to look at you, notice you. Sit by the door and jump out as he runs out. Trip him if you need to."

Would it be that simple? If he didn't acknowledge me, that was on purpose. He probably walked in and had an internal freak-out when he saw me sitting there with my legs crossed.

"You boys never went all the way, right?"

I snorted and stood to let her take the machine again. "There are degrees to that question."

"Butt stuff."

I rolled my eyes. "I played with his hole and rubbed his cock against mine, but no penetration, other than my tongue a bit. It was all mutual masturbation and me doing stuff to him. Why do I share all this with you?"

"Because I live through you, my love. Greg hasn't touched me in weeks. I think there's another woman."

"It's Greg. Of course, there's another woman. Ditch his ass."

"Says the man pining over his toxic dickweed of an ex."

"I'm not pining, and Raj isn't my ex."

"Sure thing. Let me see your sketchbook after next week, por favor."

***

As she suggested, I traded spots with Wine Granny, who was more than delighted with the view I offered her. Mrs. Brown entered and gave a short inspirational message about letting your muse flow. I wasn't paying attention, my eyes drilling into the closed door. It opened, and I watched Raj's gaze dart immediately to where I sat last week. His eyes closed, and his shoulders heaved a sigh. He opened them with a flicker of a grin but then looked directly at me.

Oh, he recognized me.

I watched his Adam's apple bob with a hard swallow. He set his focus forward to the awaiting chair. The robe fell with the same decisiveness, and he dropped into the pose with a leg thrown over the armrest, giving Wine Granny a minor heart attack, and an arm behind his head. The only difference was his eyes were angled toward where I sat last week.

"Omar, if you would, please," Mrs. Brown said softly. "You were looking that way. Please, for continuity."

His Adam's apple bobbed again, and he looked at me, directly at me. Last week, I might have believed he was watching some object a thousand feet beyond the community center's walls. Now he looked straight at me, focusing on me, and my cock twitched.

I tried to capture something on my sketch-pad, such as the curve of his bicep and how his hair fell over his ear. I spent more time watching his chest swell with each breath or trying to read something in his eyes.

"Some subjects are harder than others. Keep at it, Marshal," said Mrs. Brown at my shoulder, making me jump. She was already moving on when I glanced toward her.

The bell chimed, and Raj jumped up, his robe slipping over his shoulders. As he passed me, I grabbed his elbow.

"Not here," he hissed and shook from my grip.

Wine Granny stood in front of me a second later, thanking me profusely. "I was worried when I stood up that I would have left a wet spot on my chair!" she laughed, and I tried to hide my reaction with a chuckle. While she talked, I packed up my things, trying to give her a hint that I didn't want to stick around to chat, but it was still almost ten minutes before I was in the community center hallway, wondering where Raj might have gone. Maybe the locker room between the pool and workout room. He had to leave his clothes somewhere. I headed that way.

A dozen steps in that direction, a hand shot out from a cracked door, snagged my arm and yanked me in. I tried to yelp, but another hand clapped over my mouth.

In the dim supply closet, I stared into Raj's dark eyes. He slowly pulled his hand away, and the door closed with a quiet click.

"Marshal." His breath tickled my lips. "I..." He lessened his grip on my elbow, sliding up my arm, my shoulder, to cup my cheek. It was a tenderness he had never shown me before, and I leaned into it.

"I gave up on seeing you again," I said, my hands finding his hips through the soft cotton, shifting to pull him closer.

His hand slipped between us, loosening the robe's belt so it fell open.

"Raj, not here. Anyone could walk in."

"Anyone always could." His hand at my cheek laced through my hair, gripping the back of my head, and the other worked at unbuckling my jeans. "That's half the fun." He slid a hand down my front, squeezing my cock painfully.

I dove forward, pressing my lips to his, and his tongue lashed out, breaking through to tangle with mine. My hands snaked across his abs and hip to cup his ass and press him firmly so his erection stabbed against me.

"I didn't know what I wanted six years ago, Marshal. Now I do."

I didn't question why that would be me, a six at best, when he was a clear ten in any town.

Raj dropped to his knees, pulling my jeans with him. He took me in his mouth without hesitation, hollowing his cheeks while driving me to the back of his throat. He never touched me years ago, but now worked me with clearly practiced skill and determination. The hour of edging while we stared at each other meant he had me close within a minute, but he pulled off with a wet pop.

"You've changed," I said, breathless.

He stood, gripping fistfuls of my shirt. "Fuck me, Marshal," he pleaded.

"I— Why?"

"Don't you want to? Don't you ever wish we had years ago? We could have spent all of college doing everything we could think of to each other."

Oh, I had; thought of it all, that is. I gave up counting the number of times I jerked off, thinking about Raj's empty bunk beneath mine. I imagined it was him I was inside more than once while fucking a guy who wouldn't remember my name. A lot more than once.

Denying him now felt like a betrayal of all those past emissions.

Why hadn't we done more than show off for each other in our dorm room? Who had made that decision? Why did we save touching each other— or mostly me touching him— for the laundromat supply room?

"Not here, Raj. If this is going to happen after so long, I want to do it properly."

He chewed his lip but nodded. "Meet me in the parking lot in ten, and I'll follow you." He fastened his robe and peeked out the door. After a breath, he slipped barefoot into the hall.

My jeans were nearly soaked through with precum a few seconds after I pulled them up. I counted to thirty to give Raj time to create distance between us and fled the small room. It felt like an hour of standing beside my car before I saw him exiting the center's glass doors with his long jacket's collar popped high. I waved, he nodded, and we got in our cars. A few minutes later, of closely watching him in my rearview, I was unlocking my apartment.

He didn't want the tour or a refreshment. Just inside, he slammed me against the wall, hands tearing at the clothes keeping us apart, lips and tongue battling with mine. We left a breadcrumb trail of clothes to the bedroom.

Raj toppled back onto the sheets and beckoned me to join him.

Fucking hell, he was perfect. I'd been staring at his naked body for three hours over the last week. I'd thought about, fantasized about, the memory of him for years. I knew every inch of his body from the months we'd shared the apartment. But now he was grinning, wanting me like he never did before... The fire in his dark eyes...

I took my time, kissing my way from the arch of his foot, his ankle, his calves. He squirmed when I reached his knees and inner thigh. His cock stood at aching attention directly at me, begging to be touched, but I made it wait. He whimpered when I moved past to his hip bone and drew my tongue along his V, kissing each ab. His fingers wound through my hair when I licked across a perfect nipple. He hissed when I reached his clavicle and continued across his neck, along the shell of his ear.

Back to those lips, I crushed him with a kiss more fiery than what I ever gave my ex.

Our cocks slid together, wet with precum, and I reached between us to grasp them as one. I'd done this a dozen times while standing in the janitor's closet, but our cocks were always facing opposite directions, opposing. Now we lined up as I stroked us, and I did my best not to create a metaphor from that. I didn't want to finish us this way, but nor did I want to stop.

Raj decided for us, grasping my dick and pushing it down, against his hole.

The questions flooded forward again. Why now? What changed? Why me?

Instead of asking, I fumbled with the night-stand, taking out the pump of lube and a rubber. With skill developed on his old bed in our dorm, I had the condom on and slick with lube within seconds. I aligned and pressed forward.

A gasp escaped him as I breached the ring of muscle. Maybe I should have given him a moment to acclimate with a finger or two, but I held at just the tip, waiting for the tightness in his expression to lessen. When it didn't quickly enough, I pulled out and ran my fingers across his tight hole, about to slip one in.

"Don't you fucking dare," he said.

He bucked me to roll us and ended up on top. Sitting over my cock, he aligned and sat back, taking me fully in one smooth motion. Raj leaned back, bobbing his hips once. His face changed from pinched pain to wide pleasure.

This was it. I was fucking Raj Singh. Raj Fucking Singh.

I wasn't far from triple digits in the number of guys I'd fucked, but Raj Singh was the one I always wanted the most. The first one I always thought about when I needed help getting me over the line.

"That's it," he growled and lurched his hips again. His tight muscle squeezed me tip to hilt.

I took a handful of his chest in one hand and his cock in the other, his foreskin making it easier to slide along his length.

Raj shifted to a squat, riding me hard and fast, bringing me close to the edge faster than I could stop him.

Sweat shone over his perfect body while his breath came harder. He didn't slow when he tightened around me and I felt his orgasm start before the first stream of cum shot across my shoulder, hitting my chin and the pillow. His heat splashed across my chest, painting me, and I surged within him, filling the condom.

He only slowed when we were both spent. He dismounted, tore the condom off, and sucked the release from my cock, licking up my length.

It was enough that I debated being able to go again immediately. He could fuck me on the second go. Maybe in the kitchen, bent over the counter. Or in the shower. Or on the couch.

I lived alone. We could desecrate every surface, only coming up to hydrate.

Raj kissed me tenderly and crawled backward off the bed. A second later, the bathroom light clicked on, and the door closed.

I lost my virginity to him years ago in a weird, toxic relationship that lasted months and ended overnight. He was clearly unable to be his true self back then. By his skill at sucking and riding my dick, he'd clearly gotten better about it since. It was pointless to dwell on what we could have been back then, but could we have something now? There wasn't any rush today. We could figure it all out, maybe over breakfast tomorrow.

He exited the bathroom and made for the bedroom door.

"Why don't you stay the night?" I asked to his back—a back of tight muscle and a firm ass.

He stopped, one hand on the door frame, and turned. His front was even nicer to look at.

Raj finally nodded and returned to the bed-side. Was he about to run off without a word? He tossed the sheets aside to get under, and I scrambled to join him. It might be an hour earlier than I normally go to sleep, but I wasn't about to fight it. I curled up to him, spooning against his back with my nose against the base of his neck, breathing in his familiar lotions.

My cock twitched, and he shifted his hips back, pressing tighter into me. I ran my flat palm down his front, across the defined cut of unknown hours in the gym, to encircle his cock, raging hard again.

He encouraged mine back to his hole, still slick with lube, and this time, I felt his contended sigh when I slipped in. I rarely let this happen without protection, even after the first year with Jorge, but this felt right. Our bodies blended into one, and I pressed deeper.

I worked him gingerly, rubbing a thumb through the precum wetting his crown and spreading it down his length. Pushing as deep as possible, he rewarded me with a soft moan. I moved quicker, and his breath hastened to match. He rolled to face into the bed, and I matched him, mounting with one hand tangled in his hair, pushing him into the pillow while the other's nails bit into his hip.

He gasped, tightening around me, and I knew he was cumming into my sheets. That was enough to push me over the edge yet again, blasting another load into him that somehow felt like more than the first.

I collapsed onto his back, sweaty and exhausted. He heaved beneath me, trying to catch his breath. I kissed across the base of his spine to his shoulder, but he wasn't ready to roll over yet.

I pulled out after a moment, quietly shocked that I was still hard enough to penetrate if we wanted to try for a third go. Instead, I slipped into the bathroom and cleaned up without turning on the light. I came back with a towel to put over his mess to find him on his side, eyes closed, asleep.

He'd shifted from his cum stain, so I spread out the towel and laid on it, spooning him again. All my fanciful dreams starring him, which I had even while with my ex, came back in stark possibility. We'd work out the awkwardness from our past. This would all work out. The universe pulled us apart and now put us back together after giving us time to grow. I drifted to nothingness, breathing him in.

***

I woke alone. Raj's clothes were gone from where we'd scattered them the night before, and his car was gone from the parking lot. I never had his phone number.

The only thing that remained of him was his smell on my sheets. Part of me wanted to keep them on the bed despite the sex stains splashed across them. I picked up the pillow, taking a deep breath of him. Maybe he'd gone out for coffee and donuts. He'd be back soon, and I'd feel silly for thinking he'd left like he had before.

Except, he would have left last night if I hadn't invited him to stay. He'd paused in the doorway, debating between bolting and getting one more go out of me. How could I track him down again? Should I? If he kept running from me, he clearly didn't want anything to do with me.

Maybe Mrs. Brown could give me the information for his modeling agency. Would that be stalking?

Hygiene eventually won me over. By mid-afternoon, without a delivery of coffee or donuts, I stripped the bed and took everything to the laundry room to wash Raj Singh from my life again. If only I could wash him from my mind and heart with hot water and a Tide pod.

And Chill

Scott answered on the first knock. I raised my six-pack of hard ciders, and he raised a garbage bag. Nodding me into his apartment, he padded down the hall toward the trash chute. I wasn't sure what to wear for a movie night, but when he returned a moment later, I noted his worn sweats and faded comic tee matched my loose joggers and old band shirt. I was sure the kids in my class hadn't been born yet when I bought the shirt at a concert, but so what? It was comfortable. Stepping out of my Chucks, I followed Scott to the living room.

This was my first time in his place, and though he talked at work in length about his various collections, I wasn't ready for the sheer number of glass displays housing classic toys and models. Barely a square inch of drywall was visible between the vintage posters and framed first editions. The place would be worth a fortune to a collector, but I guess that was Scott in this case.

The living room couch pointed at the TV, as expected. A game controller and headset on the coffee table were pushed aside for a pizza box, and I set the six-pack beside that. Scott flipped the pizza open, snagging a slice as he fell back onto the couch. I opened a cider for each of us before taking a slice and sitting to his right, tossing a leg up on the chaise beside my cushion.

At work over the last week, we discussed and debated in lengthy detail what to watch, deciding on Deep Cover, a new action thriller starring each of our favorite actors. The internet was abuzz with it, but we both managed to avoid spoilers. All we knew was that the internet bros were up in arms, pissed about something in the movie, but their opinions weren't ones I cared about. If anything, the controversy only made me want to see it that much more. Scott selected it with one remote, picked up another from the coffee table to dim the lights, and settled back with his knee tossed over the armrest beside him, barefoot swinging.

The movie opened with a drone shot zooming through some major city's tall buildings, weaving around rooftop water towers and antennas, and pulling in tight behind a police officer scaling the steps of a brownstone. He banged on the door and was greeted by one of the leads holding a bath towel around his waist, hair and bare chest dry. Good start to a flick, with my favorite actor half-naked, and, damn, he looked nice. I'd seen as much of him nude as the internet had to offer, but he added a few extra pounds of muscle for the role. The cop pushed past him, demanding to know about some covert drug ring in what even I could tell was decidedly lousy acting. The camera finally panned around to show the officer's face and reveal that it was the other lead Scott was most looking forward to. The situation was getting heavy, and the dialogue became more heated until the cop demanded to see what was in the basement and reached for a door handle. The other tried to stop him, and the bath towel fell to the hardwood floor. Full shot of my guy's sculpted ass with the cop's eyes taking their time running over his front.

A second later, they were wrapped in each others' arms, lips pressed together in a passionate, messy kiss.

We were expecting a thriller, but this opening scene... holy fuck. No wonder this movie was breaking the internet. Two B-list celebrities getting gay. Really gay. I stole a glance beside me. Scott set his bottle on the side table and dropped his hand on his hip, stretching and adjusting the cotton. His eyes never wavered from the screen, but I saw the twitch of what grew in his groin.

My guy had Scott's pinned to the wall, tearing at the cop uniform with clumsy fingers. He stopped long enough for a close-up of running his tongue up the cop's neck. A picture on the wall at the side of the frame showed the two smiling at a beach, showing an eagle-eyed viewer that this was all a couple's role-play.

Leaving a trail of the cop costume, they ended up in the bedroom, both naked except for the police hat. Careful camera work kept the celebrities' dicks from being seen, but only barely.

Scott pulled his leg back from over the armrest, the movement catching my eye without moving my head. He adjusted the bulge in his sweats, then stroked it. He glanced at me, and I focused forward, pretending I hadn't noticed. My actor was blowing Scott's in an overhead shot from the ceiling, head bobbing and left hand working with the rhythm. I would have loved to be the intimacy coordinator on the set to know how these guys weren't actually having sex.

My dick screamed for attention, straining against the joggers.

Scott slid a hand into his sweats, doing more than a quick adjustment, stroking himself in the confines of whatever underwear he wore, if any. I still faced the movie but put as much attention on him as my hand slid to my groin to stroke a finger down to the side of my cock.

Onscreen, my guy licked and kissed his way up Scott's actor's belly, chest, and neck, pausing for an instant to stare into each other's eyes. I could fully believe they were in love and had been for years. No wonder they made fifteen million dollars a movie. They kissed passionately this time, sharing each other's breath. Foreheads and noses pressed together as one rutted against the other.

Scott pulled out his cock; his balls pressed up against his sweat's elastic. Fuck, I had to look.

Scott met my gaze, then shifted down to my crotch, then to his thick, uncut cock and shaved balls. He worked it slowly, pulling back the foreskin to draw my attention to his head, to the bead of precum on the tip.

Onscreen, glass shattered, and the guys rushed to throw on clothes. A group in black with big guns swarmed in, pinning both to the bed and dragging off my guy. The inciting incident happened in the movie, but also in Scott's living room.

We work together. Wouldn't this complicate things? Jerking off with a coworker? I'm generally a lot shyer about showing my dick to someone for the first time, especially after seeing he's a lot bigger than me, but... fuck it. I lifted my hips just enough to pull my joggers to my ankles and sat back, pulling my dick downward to slap against my belly.

His grin widened, and he leaned toward the side table, taking something from its drawer. Unscrewing the cap on a jar, he offered it first to me: coconut oil. Dipping two fingers in, I scooped out a portion. He did the same, and he set the jar aside.

We watched each other rub the solid oil over our cocks, working it to melt on our skin. Goddamn, I wanted to touch his dick, to feel what he was feeling.

He circled a finger on his head and brought it to his lips, ensuring I saw everything. He scooted an inch closer to me so our knees touched. I did the same, so our thighs pressed against each other. Scott stroked with his left hand to let his right relax on his leg between us, fingers curling naturally.

My left arm crossed the space between us to trace fingertips along the inside of his thigh. Scott pulled his cock downward to slap back against his belly, as I had, then took his hand away, meeting my gaze and pulling it toward where he wanted me to go.

Yeah, fuck it.

He gasped and shifted his hips upward with my grasp. I started a slow rhythm, pulling from his base to the tip and sliding back with a teasing, feather touch. His right hand was on me a breath later, squeezing with gentle pressure rather than stroking.

The movie was lost to both of us. The fake cop might save the man in the towel, but how he did it would take another viewing. If that were with Scott again, we'd have to fast-forward through the opening scene to ensure we actually watched it that time.

Or not. If this happened every time we tried to watch the movie, I was completely fine with that.

Scott shifted closer, hip to hip, still working me with a technique like flexing his fingers in a wave. I did the opposite to him, enjoying his full length and girth in slow, increasingly aggressive strokes. Every little moan and sigh gave me quiet permission to go harder.

The only thing keeping me from blasting a load across his living room was focusing on Scott. But that load was clearly both our goals.

His breath came quicker through parted lips, and he shifted down on the couch, pulling up his shirt at the same time. He squeezed his eyes tight with one last held breath, then let it out. His cock pulsed in my fist, arcing cum a few inches upward before coating my hand and pooling beneath his belly button.

Scott's rhythm abruptly changed to working me fast from base to tip, squeezing hard. I hadn't realized he'd brought me so close, and I barely had time to pull up my shirt before I blasted to my ribs.

Grinning, he turned back to the side table and pulled out two hand towels. He was fully prepared for anything over there. He unfurled a towel on my stomach, dragging a side to scoop up my cum. He could have just handed it to me, rather than clean me up. I was ready to give him the same service, but he did it himself before I could act, using the same towel. Scott wiped his fingers with the second clean towel before offering it to me. I wiped my hands, stomach, and cock again before passing it back. I'd need a rinse in the shower, or at least a wet wipe, to actually feel clean, but this was enough that I could pull my shirt down.

I didn't, though. I sat naked from ribs to ankles, angling my deflating cock toward my coworker in the dim overhead light and flicker of the forgotten thriller. Scott tugged on his balls, stretching the skin.

What now?

Scott leaned forward and reached over his shoulder, pulling his shirt over his head as he sat back. Next, he bridged his hips to push his sweats to his knees and bicycled his feet to work them to his ankles and off.

We already came, and the movie was lost. What was he planning here?

He ran expectant eyes over me as he threw a knee over the armrest as he had before, now fully naked in the dim living room light.

Whatever it may be, I was down for it.

I tossed my shirt on the floor, stepped out of the joggers, and pulled off my socks. Pivoting to sit on the chaise seat beside me, I positioned my legs toward Scott. Propping my left knee against the back of the couch, I let my other drop wide.

Scott watched it all. He scooped my foot into his lap, letting it rest against his cock while he rubbed my instep. I sat up again to adjust the pillows behind me, and the instant I settled, Scott crawled up me on all fours, staying low, a playful smirk glinting in his eyes. He kissed my thigh, ran his tongue from the base of my balls to the tip of my cock, kissing and nipping my belly, my ribs, a nipple, until he reached my lips. I was spent but longed for what he'd do next, shivering with the anticipation of unknown car-nal delights as he eased his weight onto me. Whatever he wanted, I was his tonight.

His breath was hot against my ear. I felt him harden against my thigh, and I tried to again his stomach.

"How about next time we play the quiet coworkers who fuck on the balcony?" he said, tickling my ear.

"Give me twenty minutes, a bottle of water, a scoop of peanut butter, and you got it." I grabbed a fistful of Scott's ass, pressing him tighter against me.

He pushed up enough to meet my gaze, squinting, trying to tell if I was bluffing. I wasn't. I don't think I was. Our record together was six times in thirty-six hours, but that had been almost ten years ago. It had been a long week, and tonight, I wouldn't mind taking turns wrecking each other on the balcony.

Lube Job

THE STACCATO CLICK OF hard leather on smooth concrete heralded her coming, irritatingly off-beat with the classic rock belting from the old radio. Tearing my eyes from the half-disassembled engine, I looked down at those Louboutins, following creamy legs a very long way until the hem of a tight black dress finally covered them. When she got that dress, I half-joked that she could wear it to a gynecologist appointment. I proved my point that night when I fucked her on the washing machine without pushing up the hem. The first time she wore it out without me, I was pissed, livid, but that didn't stop her from clicking her way out the door to the waiting Uber. Now I didn't give a shit.

"Sandi called," said the owner of that dress, speaking around her chewing gum. "Rick's being a shitbag again, and she needs a drink."

My eyes finally made it over her barely-covered tits—the doctor who gave her those was a genius at his craft—up the cross on a gold chain, past painted and contoured lips and cheeks, to meet that look my girlfriend gave me more often than not these last two months: annoyed and bored.

I looked her over again, from teased hair to four-inch heels and back up. I opened my mouth to say what I was thinking, to ask if she was meeting for drinks before or after her shift under the overpass, but I bit it back. Unfortunately, I went too long without replying, and she knew what I was doing my best not to say.

"I don't want to fucking hear it, Lance." She snapped long, painted nails in my face. "Not after what you did." A car honked at the end of the drive. She hitched her purse's thin strap a little higher on her shoulder and turned to the open garage door. "Don't wait up." Before her pilates-sculpted ass disappeared, she added, "My brother's coming over."

I ran after her, catching her elbow as she lowered herself into the backseat of the rideshare. "What the fuck, Shelly? I don't need a babysitter."

She stared at my hand on her until I let go. "Your actions say otherwise." She slipped into the car, tugging her tiny dress down as far as the fabric would allow, and was gone.

Fuck this. Last week was FitHub247's annual car show. Classics, prototypes, and everything in between. I hadn't missed one since my dad first took me twenty years ago, but I pulled something in my back, laying me up for three days. So, instead, I was scrolling Instagram from a heating pad, liking dozens of photos and wishing I'd been there. Two of those photos happened to contain an ex as the model.

Shelly took that as proof that if I wasn't already fucking Nicole again, that I desperately wanted to. And that gave her all the permission she needed to leave the house looking like a mid-class prostitute.

Standing like an asshole in the dark street, watching the taillights dwindle, sweat prickled my back and my pulse pounded down to my clenched fingertips. I focused on my breath, trying to slow down, trying to cool the heat rushing up my neck, burning my ears. I needed to get lost in the engine, lost in my work. Only that could bring me down.

That, or I needed to beat the shit out of something.

I returned to my place in front of the 1970 Corvette LT-1. I fucking loved this car, full of memories of holding on for dear life as my dad tore up the open road between Dallas and Houston. Too bad the engine died when he did.

The garage was ten degrees hotter than when I left it, and I pulled off my t-shirt, catching my bent reflection in the toolbox lid. Yeah, fuck Shelly. Any woman should want what I had to give them. These arms and chest? Fuck yes. I'm a high value man.

Headlights were coming up the driveway at me, pulling me from thinking about bending Nicole over the leather seats. I still had her number on my other phone, the one Shelly didn't know about. I should see what's up with her.

He walked through the headlights just as they automatically shut off. Bryant, Shelly's kid brother. Well, twenty-four or six, or I don't give a shit, but he still played video games and read comic books.

I turned away, flipping through the stereo's presets and finding the station with the game on.

"...Cowboys are up by 21 going into the fourth quarter..." was all I needed to hear. Maybe the night wouldn't be completely shitty.

Bryant stepped into the garage, raising a six-pack.

Maybe a little less shitty, yet.

"Hey, Lance," he said, sounding as uncomfortable as he looked in jeans, boots, a long-sleeved button-up shirt, and a cowboy hat that probably still had the tag on it. Shelly must have told him to dress to impress me. He did not.

"Hey, yourself," I grumbled, leaning over the engine again, but I didn't refuse the beer he offered me. I never bought that craft shit myself, but I wouldn't turn down a free one.

He set the others on a chair and came to my side, leaning into the engine. "Having any luck?" He tried to hide it, but I saw how he was eye fucking me. I wasn't mad. Fuck, I know I looked good. Yesterday was chest day, and I wrecked my old bench press record. If I was queer, like Bryant, I'd do anything to fuck me.

I turned, leaning against the side. Goddamn, it was hot in here. I pressed the beer to my forehead, letting him get a good look at me. Yeah, drink all this in. I was still half-chubbed from thinking about Nicole and adjusted myself through my jeans.

Bryant's Adam's apple lurched, watching my performance.

"I'll get her purring." I chugged half the beer before realizing it was some good shit, probably with a pretty high APV. If I pounded a few more and polished off the Jack in the back of the fridge, I could be passed on the couch long before Shelly clicked in at 3 am.

"What did your sister say to make you come over?" I asked, draining the rest and shaking the empty bottle.

Bryant finished his in four deep gulps and traded both of ours for fresh ones. He was a good kid. Too bad his sister could be such a bitch.

Not "could be." She was a bitch. All the time. But she was also a great lay.

"She said you did something to piss her off, that she doesn't trust you home alone, and that I'm a loser with nothing else to do on a Saturday night."

"Fucking bitch," I growled.

"Tell me something I don't know." He took off the ridiculous hat and tossed it aside.

"I don't need you here."

He ran a hand through his hair, ruffling his dark mess. "But I'm here now. Want to do something?"

I sighed and waved at the engine. "If you actually give a shit, I can tell you where I'm at in fixing this." I didn't have any hope a skinny computer nerd would be able to help, but I didn't want to kick him out until the beers were gone.

I turned to the engine, but he caught me by the wrist, pulling me back to face him. "Or," he started, letting his eyes run down my bare chest. I'd done it to a thousand women, but to have someone do it to me? Another man? Yeah, I'd posed for him a second ago, but that was different. My other fist was balled, ready to knock his teeth out as he bit his lower lip.

He jerked my wrist and brought his nose within inches of mine, daring me to hit him. "Look, Lance. You don't want me here, but here I am. How about we make the most of it?"

"Fucker, I'm not gay." I tried to shake my wrist from his grip, but goddamn he was strong. No nerd had the right to overpower me like this.

"Nothing gay about getting your dick sucked." He let go of my wrist to grab my dick through my jeans, still just as chubbed.

His little shit-eating grin dared me to hit him, his eyes locked on mine, almost begging me to resist, but I didn't. My arms were slack at my sides. Yeah, nothing gay about getting a blowjob in the garage. Thinking about fucking Nicole got me all worked up, and Shelly would deny me when she finally strolled in. A guy like me shouldn't have to take care of himself. If only Shelly came in just as I busted over her brother's face. I'd pay to see that.

Not that a guy could get me off.

Bryant unbuckled my belt, pulled it free, and tossed it around his neck. He popped the button on my jeans and slid a hand down. I got a surge in the need to hit him when his warm fingers wrapped around my cock, but I tore my eyes from him to focus on this month's Ms. Fithub. She had two fingers in her mouth, and another two spreading her pussy for the camera.

My cock twitched, almost fully hard. I stared at September's tits and her pebbled nipples as Bryant dropped to his knees, pulling my jeans with him.

His tongue moved up the underside of my cock, swirled on the tip, and sucked it once with a wet pop. He held my balls with one hand, rolling one at a time, while another finger brushed the backside of my sack. Wet warmth slid down my length, and I couldn't stop the moan. Shelly rarely gave me head and never like this. She might tease the tip, but Bryant took me to the back of his throat, working his tongue with practiced skill.

How good would Ms. Fithub be at sucking dick? I bet she was a pro. I bet she was as good as Bryant.

My hand moved on its own to run through the hair of the one going down on me. I gripped it, pushing my hips forward, taking control. He didn't resist, didn't gag, as he took everything I gave him. He could take more. My fingers found the belt around his neck, gripping it to pull him forward. He—

"Fuck!"

I yanked my hips back and raised a fist, ready to hit Bryant. No guy was going to make me come, and I was fucking close.

He jumped to his feet, grabbing my fist in one hand and my throat in the other, slamming my hips back against the car. Leaning close to my ear, he hissed, "Say her name if you want this to stop, but I bet you don't."

A fucking safeword? He was giving me a blowjob, not... I struggled against his grip, barely able to pull my hand free. His hand was still at my throat, tight enough to dim my vision at the edges, but something in that made my cock twitch a little harder.

My hand relaxed, and I blinked away tears.

"Good boy," he said and took my hand, guiding it to touch his cock.

Fucking hell. I had to look down. I don't know when he took that out, but, Christ, the girth. Curiosity made me squeeze it, try to touch my fingers around it, and gape when I couldn't. Anyone he fucked would feel it for a week. I never would have guessed this nerd kid was packing this much heat.

"You want my fat cock?" he whispered, his voice two octaves deeper than usual.

I swallowed hard, not sure what he meant by that and not sure why I wasn't kicking him the fuck out of my garage.

I could end it by saying her name. No. That would give her power.

I could knock Bryant's lights out or try to. His strength seemed supernatural, or something about him weakened me. Was the beer poisoned? No, he'd drunk just as much.

My lack of response was enough for him. He tossed my belt around my neck and gripped my hair, pushing me down. I've put guys in the hospital for touching me, but now Bryant's massive cock was in my face as I kneeled before him.

"Lick it," he ordered.

I looked down at my cock standing rigid between my thighs, feeling for the first time like I wasn't enough. A skinny kid had me feeling helpless, bowing before something I could never measure up to.

"Lick it or say her name," he said, voice deep and even.

I wouldn't give her that power over me.

His fingers tightened, forcing me to focus forward, and I licked the underside of his cock as he had mine. I expected to gag or hurl, but there wasn't much to it. Why did it take so much goddamn work to get a girl to do this? I followed the thick vein along it to the crown and gagged when I tasted his salty-sweet precum.

"Keep going," he said, and his fingers relaxed.

I finished my beer, rinsing the taste of him from my mouth, and set the bottle beside the tire.

His pubes were trimmed neatly, and his shaved balls hung heavy. I touched that soft skin, and he hissed as it tightened. The angry red crown stared at me, wet with his precum and my spit. It didn't taste that bad; I just wasn't ready for it. Had I ever tasted my own cum? Not in a long time. Maybe a decade ago.

His fingers twitched. Bryant took one end of the belt, threaded it through the buckle, and tightened it around my throat.

I licked up his length and around the head, wondering if I could even get it all in my mouth at once.

Why would I want to do that?

Because now I was curious, and why shouldn't I? I was a goddamn man. I could do whatever the fuck I wanted to.

Wrapping one hand as best I could around the base of his shaft, I stretched my lips around the head. He filled my mouth, choking me before he was halfway past my tongue, yet he had another hand span left.

"Breathe," he said, taking my hair again in a fist while tugging on my leash. He pulled his hips back and rocked slowly forward.

"Play with yourself," he said, and I did. My cock hadn't been this hard since I was a teenager, the tip dripping a stream of precum to the concrete floor. The barest touch brought me close to the brink. My view of his massive cock and tidy pubes blurred with tears as he pressed deeper with each thrust. He said I only had to say her name to make this all end, but how could I say anything with him filling me, making it impossible to breathe?

I couldn't last. I felt it in my balls, pinching the base of my skull down to my taint. I must have moaned, giving myself away.

"Do it, Lance. Let it go."

I gasped around his cock, and he held me onto it with a hand pressing against the back of my skull. It kept me from collapsing forward with the first pulse. Pump after pump, it felt endless, and he held me there, pegged in place.

He finally let go when I was done releasing across the floor, allowing me to gasp for air. With a firm fist in my hair, he tilted my head back to look up at him with bleary eyes.

"Good boy, Lance. We're almost done."

He wiped my eyes with his free hand, and I let him, clearing my view of him. I always saw Bryant as a skinny twerp until that moment. He was powerful, standing over me, and he took his cock with the other hand with slow strokes.

I flinched with the first shot across my cheek. My lips parted for the third. My tongue extended for the fifth as he painted me. It was in my eyes, in my hair.

Blinded, I felt him squat in front of me.

"Let me know when you get sick of my sister."

He ran a hand across my cheek to the back of my head, smearing cum through my hair, and his lips were on mine.

I wiped the mess from my eyes and squinted them open, barely able to see more than shadows as he took up the cowboy hat and left the garage. Headlights flashed, and he backed out of the driveway.

I was sprawled against my car, naked with my jeans around my ankles, heaving to catch my breath with my belt around my neck, my face covered in another man's cum. What the fuck just happened, and why wasn't I mad about it? I wiped my eyes again.

Why wasn't I mad?

"...Cowboys are on their way to an undefeated season..."

Why did I want it to happen again?

Payback

I KNOCKED TWICE AND hefted the backpack up my shoulder. I packed light for the weekend trip, but the straps were digging in after the two-mile walk from the train station and hiking up ten flights. I had a thing against elevators.

He called out on the other side of the door just as I raised my fist to knock again.

"It's open!"

This would be fine, yeah? Markus and I last saw each other ten years ago, and we weren't particularly close back then. Crashing on his couch would save a small fortune on a hotel. Even if this was about to be the most awkward few days, we could just ignore each other if we had nothing in common. I had a ridiculous crush on him the last time I saw him, and he... Well, he didn't treat me that well. Time tends to soften most things, at least I hoped.

Just inside, I pulled off my shoes to sit beside his, which were at least three sizes larger. Sunlight flowed in through the wall of windows on the far side of the studio apartment, looking out at another building across the street. Sparse furniture dotted the floor: a dark gray couch piled with bedding and a plush bed peeking from behind a floral privacy screen. Three stools were tucked up against the bar that separated the kitchen from the rest of the space. A clatter of pots drew me closer to the bar. My host popped up with a tray in his oven mitts. He could have been one of the dozen bakers I followed on Instagram with broad, bare shoulders under his dark red apron.

"You're early." Markus set down the tray of oatmeal cookies and tossed back a blonde lock. "I haven't showered or set up your bed yet."

"Yet you had time for cookies." I leaned my elbows on the cold marble to peek at him, pretending to better see the treats. Every muscle popped from where he stood barefoot in his kitchen, possibly naked behind the apron.

"I had to make cookies for my baby brother," Markus grinned.

I rolled my eyes. "We're not brothers. Our parents were barely married."

"Close enough." Markus took off the mitts and left the kitchen, giving me a brief view of loose gray shorts under the apron. He came up beside me, arms wide for a hug. "Welcome to Chicago. It's great to see you."

I accepted the embrace, letting him enfold me in powerful arms.

With my nose at his neck, smelling his after-shave and the cooling cookies, I couldn't reconcile him with memories of our past. Markus had been terrible to me in the brief months we lived together while my dad and his mom were married. Every sort of shitty older brother bullying, he did it. My hands moved across his bare back, and I tried not to notice the firmness there.

He pushed me back to arm's length with his hands still on my shoulders. "You got big, Tom. Do you work out or play a sport?"

I shrugged. "No. I work in construction. What about you?" Asking gave me an excuse to slide a palm down his bicep and squeeze.

"Gym and..." he coughed and winked. "Home workouts."

I noticed that he had no exercise equipment, so I guessed what he meant by that.

"How about lunch?" Markus asked, adjusting his thin, wireframed glasses.

"Yeah, sure." I wasn't hungry, but whatever.

He untied the apron, hanging it on a hook inside the kitchen, leaving his chest bare. Hair dusted his pecs to the barbells shining from his nipples. The trail continued beyond the low waistband of his shorts. Shorts with a clear outline of a thick cock.

"I'll grab a quick shower, and we'll run out," he said, his eyes trailing over me before disappearing behind the privacy screen.

My cock strained against my jeans, but I tried to ignore it and flopped on the couch, leaning back against the pile of sheets, blankets, and pillows with my knees over the armrest. I unlocked my phone to browse for restaurants nearby when another phone buzzed on the coffee table.

Markus jogged up beside me and snatched it. He answered and took the conversation back behind the screen, but his whispered words were clear in the open floor plan.

"Hey... Yeah, he just got here... I don't know, like I remember him, but fucking stacked..." He snorted a laugh. "Fuck off, man... Yeah... Yeah, we'll see about that... Yeah, later."

I scrambled to look busy on my phone when Markus stepped around the side of the couch again. With a thin white towel wrapped low around his hips, he leaned in between my knees over the armrest. One hand squeezed my thigh. "Sorry about that. I'll be ready in a few." He strode to the bathroom, and I watched every step of it. He worked the towel free, giving me a brief view of his toned ass before kicking the door mostly closed behind him.

Only mostly.

The water started a few seconds later, and I jumped to my feet.

There were no shadows for me to hide in the apartment, but I hoped the wire-rimmed glasses on the bathroom counter meant his vision wouldn't reach me as I leaned close to the door.

I could see every inch of his backside reflected in the mirror while he tested the water spraying in the clear glass shower. He stepped under the full force, sweeping his hair back, arching his back to let the water sluice down his chest, and he turned. His cock hung heavy, partially chubbed. His hands slid over his skin, moving without hurry.

My cock pressed against my jeans, and without thinking, I unzipped my fly to let it free.

I worked myself slowly while Markus lathered shampoo, raking it through his hair. He rinsed, and I rubbed a thumb through the precum leaking from my tip.

Markus squeezed body wash the color of creamy honey into a sponge and rubbed it across his chest. Rivers of bubbles flowed through his chest hair, following the trail to settle in his trimmed pubes. One hand worked the sponge, and the other explored his body, wrapping around his shaft, now as hard as mine. What I wouldn't give to be on my knees catching that water running off him.

I popped my button fly and pushed my jeans halfway to my knees. My right hand cupped my balls, tickling the soft skin behind them while my other worked in time with Markus. He set the sponge back, still oozing with lather and pushed a soapy hand past his cock, past his balls hanging low, to play with his ass. His brow tensed, then relaxed when he slipped inside.

He leaned back against the glass, working himself from both sides. I couldn't keep up, my knees weakening.

What if he looked up and saw me in the mirror, peering in through the door? From baking almost naked to his unquiet conversation to flashing his ass on the way into the bathroom, I was sure he'd invite me in or continue his show.

Keeping the hand between his legs to toy with his ass, his other slid up his body, achingly slow, feeling every inch of his abs and chest, to close around his throat.

I was three strokes from blasting my release across the doorjamb.

No, stop it! I couldn't make a mess right here! I jerked my hands from my cock.

His eyes snapped open, and he paused his motions as a slow grin spread over his lips. Markus quickly rinsed and grabbed another towel hanging beside the glass shower door.

I fumbled my throbbing cock back into my pants and scrambled to the couch, trying to look casual. The bathroom door swung open seconds later. Markus rubbed the towel down his chest and tossed it around his waist, pulling the thin material tight across his erection. He pushed his glasses on and crossed to stand beside me.

"I'll be ready in five," he said, squeezing my knee. The towel didn't look big enough to stay on without him holding it at his hip, and I would be fine if he didn't bother with the modesty. "I hope you're hungry."

I touched the back of his calf and drew my fingers up his knee to the back of his thigh. "Famished."

Rather than slipping back around the couch, away from my touch, he moved in front of me so my hand slid around his leg, under the towel, across his other firm thigh, an inch from those low balls.

It couldn't be clearer what we both wanted. I could have tugged him down onto me on the couch, but I let him slip away to the bedroom. I craned my neck to watch him go behind me, again losing the towel before there was a layer of privacy between us.

I wished I'd worn underwear. A wet spot was forming in my crotch from precum. My balls ached. I'd need release here soon if I hoped to be able to walk much more in the next days. My finger was absently tracing my length through the jeans, which didn't help.

Minutes past, and I debated running to the bathroom. It would only take a dozen strokes looking at the shower, imagining it was my hand around his neck and my dick where his finger had been; spreading waves of pleasure and pain through him. Lunch would be awkward with a raging boner and swollen balls. I had to do something. I stood up, squeezing myself through the jeans, assuring my cock it wouldn't have to wait much longer.

"Hey, Tom. Can you give me a hand in here?" Markus called from behind the privacy screen, no louder than he'd spoken on the phone.

I stepped around the screen, where Markus was sitting up in the king-sized bed, leaning against the headboard with the comforter pulled up across his stomach. He patted the space beside him, and my eyes went from it to the barbells studding his nipples to his hair, still wet and slicked back.

I tried to keep my cool as I sat, but my heart pounded in my throat. "How can I help?"

Markus grabbed a fist full of the comforter and tossed it aside, showing me his full glory. I just wanted to run my tongue up the thick vein on the underside of his fat cock. I wanted to lick the droplets that clung to the hair on his legs. I wanted to suck the bead of moisture from his nipple.

His hand shot out, grabbing my shirt and tugging me close. "Make me feel it in the morning."

He yanked me hard, toppling me onto him. His lips were on mine, and my tongue pushed between his. His hands worked across my heated back. I shifted to put my body between his legs without breaking our kiss. My palms ran from his thighs up his hips, his ribs, and back down. I could taste him all day, but I wanted more.

My kisses trailed down his jaw, his collarbone. I took time to suck each nipple, relishing his gasp when I bit the piercing. His ribs to his belly button, moving to press my lips along his hip bone and following the trail inward.

His cock twitched when I reached it, preparing for what I might do to it. Markus moaned with my single slow lick from base to tip.

It twitched again, flexing, begging for more.

Not yet. He teased me plenty as kids. Payback's a bitch.

I shoved my arms under his knees, pushing them to his chest, and dove forward. He gave me a gasp when my tongue moved over his puckered hole and up his taint to the base of his sack. Smooth and soft; Markus was a man who kept things tidy. I lapped him up until my tongue ached. When I thought I might have to pause, his moans reinvigorated me.

His fingers snaked through my hair and tightened, urging me on and pressing me harder into him.

My cock screamed from the confines of my jeans. I worked the fly, letting my member thump heavily onto the sheets.

An index finger gave my tongue reprieve, renewing his moan as I got past the second knuckle to press against that soft spot in him. His puckered hole glistened with my spit and I pulled out just enough to add another finger when one felt too easy.

"Bottom drawer."

I looked up and followed where he was pointing to a chest of drawers against the far wall. Not knowing what he wanted me to retrieve, but assuming I'd know it when I saw it, I pushed back off the end of the bed and pulled off my pants before crossing to and opening the bottom drawer.

There was a cookie tin full of assorted condoms, pumps of lube, bottles of massage oil, butt plugs, dildos of all sizes and varying realism, but I went for the sheen of metal and leather.

"Kinky fuck," Markus cooed and swung his legs off the bed. I untangled the straps and held it for him to step into the harness, pulling the leather taut across his chest and tightening the straps over his shoulders. Thin metal chains dangled across his ribs from the ring between his pecs to the one on his back.

"You ready to feel this?" I growled and squeezed the base of my cock.

Markus dropped onto the mattress, flipping to face me with his knees wide.

"Not here." I grabbed the harness across his chest, dragging him off the bed and tossing him past the privacy screen. He stumbled, laughing as he caught himself on the edge of the couch.

I tore my shirt over my head while stalking toward him. There was no plan. Would I fuck him? Make him suck my cock? I would have never called myself a petty person, but the guy who treated me like shit for months was now bared, naked before me, save for a leather harness.

Sometimes, no plans were the best kind.

I stood toe to toe with him, looking up into hazel eyes behind his glasses, our cocks pressed together. And I shoved him backward, over the back of the couch, to tangle in the stacked sheets and pillows. He recovered quickly, jumping to his feet and pushing his glasses in place. His grin never wavered.

Fuck him on the couch? That didn't feel right still.

My gaze flicked past him to the wall of windows and the apartments or offices across the street.

He followed my eyes, and the grin widened. Markus padded toward them, watching me the whole time. "We'll give the old lady on the eighth floor another heart attack." He spread his hands on the glass and leaned his hips toward me.

I took the bait, sliding a hand around his hip and low across his belly, then lower, taking his cock in a firm grip. It had happened too fast in the bedroom, I hadn't had time to appreciate the thrill of touching him for the first time. Now I bent him downward and squeezed, sensing how far he could move, as hard as he was.

My cock slid against his crack, and he pushed into it.

"You really want this?" I asked.

He moaned a yes.

I took him in an iron grip, moving fast along his length. "What will the old bitch across the street think seeing your seed dripping down the window?"

His breath came faster, deeper. He was close already. "Stop teasing and do it," he moaned.

Oh no, only because you asked.

I pulled his hips farther from the window, grabbed the harness to bend him forward, and worked his cock harder, faster.

"You're gonna make me—" He tried to stand, but his muscles were glamor from the gym. Mine were from manual work. He strained, but it was worthless.

Markus pressed his forehead against the glass and cried out with his first shot arcing to the window. He spat a stream of curses with every pump that followed.

I scooped my hand across his crown and spread it down my cock as lube.

Markus turned, anger evident in his eyes. "I thought you were going to make me feel—"

My hand caught him by the throat, squeezing just enough to know I'd go harder if he wanted me to, and pushed him back against the glass, against his dripping cum. His expression softened.

"Kneel," I said.

He did, taking off his glasses.

With my cock slick with his cum in one hand, I threaded the other through his hair, tilting his head back. Markus opened his mouth and extended his tongue.

That invitation was all I needed to kick me over the edge I'd been skirting since seeing him in the apron. I missed his mouth on the first three shots, hitting his eye and hair. He didn't care, greedily licking cum from his lips with every pulse. I didn't let go until the last aftershock passed.

I staggered back, looking over Markus, the mess down the window behind him, and the apartment windows across the street. If I'd gone too far, I really didn't care.

"Can I get up?" Markus asked.

I pulled him up by the harness. "Clean this up later. I want to go eat."

Markus nodded enthusiastically and rushed to the bathroom, still not closing the door.

I gathered my clothes, completely confounded by what just happened. What had come over me? Maybe it was the harness. Markus acted like he didn't remember anything he did to me a decade ago, and maybe he didn't. Maybe it didn't matter. But I caught a glimpse of his bare skin in the bathroom and knew I'd give him what he wanted before I left. I'd give him everything I ever wanted to give him years ago.

I'd make him feel it in the morning.

The Cabin

"FIFTY BUCKS SAYS AT least one person has been murdered in there," Nick said as we pulled into the rough gravel driveway. I wouldn't take that bet. The cabin was a conglomeration of every horror movie set. A creaky porch with a broken swing wrapped around to the side facing the lake. A young tree too big to be called a sapling grew too close to the slat siding, pushing at it. The front door and windows looked stout, though.

I turned off my old Ford Ranger, double-checking the address for the fifth time. "How old were the pictures on the listing?" I asked, thinking of the quaint cabin we found online, which boasted easy access to kayaking and some of the best hiking trails in the state.

"Ten years, at least. No wonder it was so cheap."

"We drove five hours, might as well check it out. We just need a place to sleep and shit."

Nick was already lifting the cooler out of the truck bed, his arms bulging like I hadn't noticed from him in the seven years since we'd met. His new job at the landscaping company must be working him out.

I carried our bags and almost ran into Nick's back when he stopped on the steps.

"What is it?" I asked.

He raised his head with a deep breath. "You hear that?"

I strained but heard nothing except the wind through the trees. I shook my head.

"Exactly. This will be perfect. Thanks, bud."

"What better way to forget your bitch girlfriend than a quiet weekend of beer and trails?"

"Fuck yeah. Fuck Shelly."

"Fuck her, indeed. I mean, not really, the skank."

I set down a bag to free up my right hand, groping behind a pot for the key. When I found it and pushed it into the lock, the door swung inward without needing it.

"Great security," I muttered.

"Great that it's not needed."

The living room took up the front half of the cabin, with two couches lifted straight from the seventies and a moose head over the fireplace. The kitchen was just a sink with an equal amount of counter space beside it and a minifridge. I could fit in the shower, but Nick would have to slouch. The two bedrooms were each barely large enough to accommodate the full-size beds.

We picked our rooms, threw our stuff down, and were changed and ready for a hike ten minutes later, complete with long pants and tick spray.

Nick led the way, rarely saying anything. I couldn't tell if his silence stemmed from a quiet appreciation of nature or a seething anger about his ex. He and Shelly had been together for two years. I pointed out her worst red flags but kept the others quiet. Nick had the ring bought, contrived the most romantic setting he could muster, dropped to a knee, and learned she'd been married the whole time. Bitch broke my best friend's soul, and all I could do was be there for him.

I followed him through tight trees, across a shallow stream, through an ancient cemetery, and along a sandy ridge with a sharp drop to waters below. It didn't all make sense with our cabin beside the still lake, but I trusted Nick's sense of direction. For hours, I watched his feet and calves, careful of where I stepped, trying not to think too hard about how much Nick had slimmed down and bulked up in the last months. I was by no means in bad shape, but my calves didn't pop like his.

When the cabin finally came into view again, my GPS reported we'd hiked thirteen miles. My feet screamed to be free of the shoes. I knew once I sat down, I'd be down for the night.

"Hop in the lake?" Nick asked, already moving toward it.

Our cabin had a shockingly solid dock poking into the water. Nick ripped off his shoes, and I plopped beside him to do the same. As I peeled off my long-sleeve shirt, I knew I wouldn't be putting any of this back on, as soaked in sweat as it was. No matter; the cabin was fifteen feet away.

"What're we doing tonight?" Nick asked, pulling my attention to him as he tugged his shirt off. I guess I'd notice how he filled up a t-shirt, but Nick was just a massive guy. Broad shoulders, pecs...

I cleared my throat. "Dogs and beers around the fire?"

"Perfect." He flashed a grin and dropped his pants. He held his arms out in a T and spun a slow circle in his boxers. "Tick check."

Scanning him from the toes up, that odd wave of jealousy hit me. I always knew Nick hit the genetic lottery that made it easy for him to build and keep muscle, but the hair across his chest and down his stomach looked perfectly sculpted, yet I knew he didn't do anything for it. This was just him.

"You're good," I said. More than good...

He beckoned me to stand, and I did, dropping my hiking pants. I felt tiny before him as Nick put his hands on my shoulders. As he shuffled me to a slow turn, a wave of jealousy of another sort struck me, something more like anger. Shelly and a handful of women before her came into this man's life and gave him hope for a future before shattering him. None of them deserved Nick.

Before I completed my thought, he declared me tick-free and jumped into the water. I was in before his cannonball's waves settled, the chill shocking my muscles that were still registering what I'd done to them on the hike today.

Both starving and exhausted, we weren't in long before Nick was hauling himself up the ladder with me right behind him. The water weighed down his boxers, flashing his full ass to everyone on the lake, which was only me. I laughed and shoved on his bare cheek, not intending to squeeze. But I did, and he didn't seem to notice while snickering and hiking up his underwear. Fading fast, we each got in a beer, but the fire didn't happen, so dinner was a protein bar. My legs were giving out when I crawled into bed. I pulled the thin sheet up to my ribs, stretched my legs, and was out.

Hissing woke me, but I was more confused than alarmed.

"Pete! I can't sleep in my bed."

I pushed to my palms. "What?"

"I can't sleep in my bed," Nick repeated. I could just make out his silhouette filling the doorway.

"I heard you. Why not?"

"Spiders."

Valid. I wasn't about to play twenty questions about what was wrong with the living room couches, so I rolled over and lifted the sheet. Nick filled the bed a second later, pushing me against the wall.

"Thanks," he whispered.

I was cramped, but it felt good, cozy.

"Yep. Night." His warmth melted into my back and lulled me back to sleep.

I needed to pee and reluctantly opened my eyes. I lay on my left side, my hand across Nick's stomach, and the sheet twisted around his thighs. Watching the slow rise and fall of his chest, that anger returned, directed at the women who'd wronged his man over and over. He deserved so much better, someone who would treat him with dignity, respect, and maybe even reverence. Whoever that person was, I'd be there when they met. I'd witnessed all his failed relationships from start to finish, so why not the one that worked out? My hand was still across his stomach, and I gave it a squeeze.

Right, bladder.

Moving carefully not to wake him, I arced my leg over Nick, feeling for the floor. I pushed to hover over him, our boxers brushing, but paused at seeing how peaceful he looked in the soft glow of moonlight. Hearing him talk about Shelly the last few years, I doubted he ever looked this restful with her. The two were constantly bickering, but he insisted they loved each other.

No. Nick and I loved each other. It was a different love, but real.

I completed my maneuver, successfully removing myself from the bed without waking him.

An old nightlight lit the tiny bathroom between the bedrooms. I fished my dick out of my boxers, only to be shocked at being hard. Not just a little chubbed, but to the point it hurt to bend my dick down to point at the bowl. It had been a few days; maybe I just needed to beat off. I could be quick and quiet.

Boxers around my ankles, the first squeeze and stroke pulled a gasp from my lips, and I leaned my ass into the cold ceramic of the sink counter. When was I last this hard? Everything felt enhanced as I gripped just below the head and pushed down, imagining nothing in particular as I usually did, focusing only on the pleasure. It wouldn't take me long, only a few strokes, but the bed creaked.

Hand covering my cock, I peeked around the corner into the bedroom. I expected Nick to be getting out of bed for the same reason I had— at least my original reason— but he'd only rolled to his side, facing away from me. That familiar tingle started at the base of my skull, spreading across my brain and down my spine, and I realized I was still stroking while watching Nick's shoulder move with his breath. The curve of his strong back down to the low waist of his boxers...

I clapped my other hand over the head to catch the first shot of my heat. Seven more followed, and I rested my head against the door-jamb to slow my breath. Hoping I caught it all, I rinsed my hands in the sputtering bathroom sink.

Palms resting on the counter, I stared into the mirror with the weak nightlight at my side. What would Nick say if he knew I'd just jerked off watching him sleep? Is that what just happened? I was already started and happened to glance his way. But I kept looking at him. I might have thought about his bare ass flashing me as he got out of the lake or how it felt to wake with my hand across his stomach. In fact, I definitely did, along with imagining his quirky grin and strong hands on my shoulders as he scanned me for ticks. I knew I loved my friend, but when had this lust started? Or was it always there?

I was too tired and sore to have an existential crisis in the bathroom at four in the morning. I'd gone down enough to pee and, within a minute, was planning my acrobatic maneuver to get back into bed. Nick had rolled to almost the middle, but I wanted back on his far side, by the wall. One leg over... Shift my weight... Feel my balls brush against this hip...

He snorted, eyes snapping open, rolling to his back and almost tossing me, but I caught myself with hands on his obliques, resting my weight down on him. I could feel his cock against my ass through our thin boxers. Was he chubbed? Fuck. I never noticed all this before tonight.

"Pete, what are you doing?"

"I had to pee." How I wished there was more light. What if I leaned forward right now and kissed him? What would he do?

There was that grin. He put a hand on my thigh, pushing me toward the far side of the bed. "You don't have to be Paul Hamm; just wake me up and tell me to move my ass."

"I'm flexible." I flopped beside him, back against the wall.

"Yeah, you are." He rolled to face me, scooting toward the far edge of the bed this time. The grin faded to a somber biting of the lip. "Hey, uh... Thanks for setting this up. I didn't realize how much I needed it; to get away. I don't know what I did to deserve a friend like you, Pete."

Saying "you're welcome" didn't feel like enough, so I said nothing. Heads on the lumpy pillow, we stared into each other eyes until I noticed the wetness threatening to slide across his nose. I wiped it away with a thumb.

"Fuck." He shoved a palm across his face, pushing the heel into his eyes. "Sorry, dude." He sniffed.

I let my hand skim his side before pulling it back between us. He was hurting, vulnerable, but fuck if it didn't feel nice to touch him, comfort him.

The grin returned. He brushed gentle, calloused fingers around my ear, down my neck, and along my side. "Feels nice," he breathed. He rested his hand between us, beside mine.

Yes, it did, but I wanted him to say it. "What feels nice?" I asked.

"All this. Being here. With you. You've always been right there, but things feel... I don't know. I could have done this anytime, but I didn't know I'd like touching you so much."

I ran my palm from his shoulder down his arm, letting my fingers shift to explore the texture of his muscles. Every slow inch quickened my breath. My fingers slipped around his palm, lifting his hand to rest on my ribs, inviting him to touch me. Back up his arm and down his side, I gripped him near the waist as leverage to scoot an inch nearer.

"So, you've wanted this too?" he asked while his fingers tickled my ribs and slipped around to press against the small of my back. He shifted closer until I could swear I felt his erection brushing against mine. If I hadn't taken care of myself ten minutes before, I would have shot right then.

I'd had my left arm cocked up under the pillow, but now I pushed it under his neck and around as my other held him tight. I shot forward, closing the tiny gap between us. Hip to hip. Stomachs, chests, and foreheads pressed together. Our breath coming deep and fast. Sweat breaking out between us. His cock stabbed into mine, and as much as I wanted to see and touch that, I wanted his lips more. More than even that, I wanted to tell him everything. My sudden realization of feelings left repressed for years. I—

He surged forward, soft lips pressing hard against mine, alternating delicate and vicious.

I matched him, tongue working against and around his. His big hand was down my boxers, holding one ass cheek, massaging it in time.

Tossing a knee over him, I rolled on top, urging him to his back. Pushing up, I savored how his cock pressed between my legs, against my taint, as I ground my hips against it. I'd never bottomed before, but I knew I would for him. No matter his size, we'd make it work for me to feel him deep in my core. Maybe not tonight, but someday soon.

Diving down, I met his waiting lips before trailing mine across his jaw and down his neck. To his collarbone and chest. His hands slid up my thighs, under my boxers, and those calloused fingers gripped my cock. It almost undid me, almost brought me to a second coming, but I needed to see him first. Meeting his dark gaze once more, I pressed one more kiss before shifting down, pulling my cock from his grip.

His was already pushed through the boxer's fly. I stroked him as I would myself, using touch to gauge his size in the dim light, guessing we were about the same. I half expected him to be massive, based on the size of the rest of him, but breathed a silent sigh of relief that I'd be able to take him. Nick's gasp turned into a moan and back to a gasp. His breath quickened, driving me to work faster, to squeeze harder. I curled forward, pushing back the foreskin to take him into my mouth. Once, twice... Each long stroke made him wetter, letting me go a little deeper. His sweet precum coated my tongue and he tasted wonderful.

Nick sucked in a quick breath and bucked, tossing me to my side. His hands on my hips, positioned between my knees, he pushed me to my back and tore off my boxers. Holding my cock in one hand, he dragged his tongue from behind my balls and up my length. No force on earth could stop the gasp that escaped me as he plunged my cock to his tonsils. I ran one hand through his hair, gripping it into a fist as he worked. For a man I'd watched fail at so many relationships with women, he sure knew how to work a cock. He brought me to the edge, ready to push me off for the second time in an hour.

He noticed my quick, shallow breathing, trying to delay the moment.

"Cum for me," he said around a mouthful.

I let go, letting that tingle wash over me, build behind my balls, and blast forward. Nick grabbed tight to my hip, catching and swallowing everything I offered him. With the last spasm fading, he licked across my head and kissed his way to my lips again. He was gentler now, more relaxed.

"Your turn," I said, sliding my hands behind his thighs, urging him nearer.

A quick flash of confusion washed over his face before that grin returned. Moving on his knees, he straddled my chest. He looked like a mountain above me. A mountain with a cock I wanted more of. So I raised my head to take him in, stretching my mouth wide.

I couldn't do much in the position, but he slid one hand behind to support my head, and the other braced against the wall. His hips started a slow wave, sliding him halfway in before pulling out. As his breathing accelerated, so did his rhythm while remaining mindful not to choke me on his girth. I wanted more. Wanted to take him deeper down my throat. Wanted to taste every inch of his skin. Wanted to lean naked against him under a blanket and watch the sunrise.

His breath caught, and he came, shooting a hot river down my throat. I held it against my tongue, savoring his flavor.

He finally calmed enough to pull from me, moving slowly to meet my lips again.

"Thank you," he said. With him between my thighs, I felt his cock stroke against my asshole. "Have you ever bottomed before?" His cock, still mostly hard, flexed against me.

My breath caught. Grinding on his hips, I told myself we'd find a way to do exactly that. I convinced myself I could take him when I finally wrapped a hand around him. But after how he filled my mouth, I worried what else he'd do to me. I could tell he was holding back as he thrust into me... I'd heard that bottoming hurt if not done right, and how could we do it right with no experience?

I shook my head.

Disappointment, then the grin returned. "Dang, I was hoping for tips. I was kind of thinking I wanted to try it and see what it felt like. I want to feel that with you." He kissed my nose, my cheek, the curve of my jaw.

Wait... "You want me to fuck you?"

My shock must have come off as something like disgust. He shied back. "No! No, I'm just... Nothing." He added an awkward chuckle and pressed himself farther from me.

I wrapped my arms around him, pulling him back to me. "I mean, I'm a bit tired right now, but I'm free all day tomorrow."

"You have no idea how long I've thought about this, Pete. Fantasized about us." Nick settled on his side and put his head on my chest. His fingers traced whorls and lines across my stomach.

"You could have fooled me with the string of Shellys." I kissed the top of his head.

"Smokescreens." His gentle pattern tickling my skin moved to my inner thigh, brushing the side of my scrotum and down my length.

His slow prodding might have stirred me for a third time, but I wanted to see him in the light of day. I settled my arms around his shoulders and squeezed. I'd only just realized my long ache for my best friend, but he'd known about and hidden his for years. What could we be like to each other after we left this cabin in a week? No one would bat an eye if we got an apartment together. This could work.

Nick's palm was settled low across my waist, and his breathing was the slow, deep rhythm of sleep. Worries for whatever we'd be after this week could wait. There was a lot of time between then and now.

Room Service

THE SUN HAD LONG set by the time I finally got to the hotel. The driver popped the trunk but didn't look up from his phone. Something caught my foot, and I tumbled from the backseat. I would have landed on the curb if not for the wall of white linen I fell against. I pushed back, catching the gleam of silver off the polished nameplate.

Raul.

Realizing my hands were flat on his chest, I jumped back.

"You okay?" he asked. He ran his tongue over his teeth as his eyes ran over me.

"Yeah, I... thanks." I adjusted the messenger bag across my shoulder and followed Raul up the three steps to the glass doors. He dragged my gaudy plaid luggage behind him and pulled the door open for me.

"Welcome to The Ace," he said with a wink. I let my gaze travel over him as I passed with a smile. His short, dark hair, dark eyes, and day-old stubble made him cute. His white shirt with three buttons undone, framing a copper ring on a necklace laying on his smooth, tanned chest, made him hot.

The young woman working behind the counter plastered on a smile when she saw me approaching with the bellhop close behind.

"Welcome to The Ace. I'm the night manager, Martina. Checking in?"

"Yes. Reservation under Lopez."

Raul leaned across the cool granite counter, crossing his arms and watching the exchange.

Her fingers danced over the keyboard. "We have you for two nights. We upgraded you to a preferred room, and I see we have your corporate card on file."

Raul's brows twitched. He rested his chin on his arms, looking like a puppy dog waiting for a treat.

"I just need a card for incidentals," said Martina.

I handed her my company gold card and bit back my grin, watching Raul's hips move with whatever beat was going on in his head. Adorable.

Martina typed a few more things, programmed a keycard, wrote my room number on its sleeve, and slid it across the counter.

"You're all set, Mr. Lopez. Take the elevator to the third floor; your room is the last on the right. The rooftop pool is open from ten to seven, and our restaurant next door, Pink Boi Tacos, has happy hour specials from three to six. If you have any questions or issues, please call or come down." Her grin returned.

I reached down for my bag, but Raul snapped to attention. "I'll show you the way, señor," he said, stabbing the elevator call button.

I thought I caught Martina rolling her eyes, but her customer service grin was fully in place when I glanced back at her.

"The company gold card, you must be doing some important business," Raul said when the doors closed, leaving us alone in the elevator car. Trapped with him, I breathed in his coconut scent. His hips never stopped moving with a beat heard only to him.

"I don't know how important it is," I said. "My firm is looking to buy another in town, and I'm here to audit their finances—or at least start the audit process."

Raul stared at me, nodding along, but his eyes belied his lack of interest.

"Any good restaurants I should hit?" I asked.

He lit up with the question as the doors slid open on the third floor. "Do you like spicy?" He waggled his eyebrows.

"That depends on my evening plans," I waggled back.

He bit his thumb, considering me. "You're going to get me in trouble, señor. Try Paulo's on 18th. The ceviche is," he kissed his fingers and exploded them out. "Their salads and fruit bowls are good, too, if that's what you need." He winked.

At the last room on the right, Raul tapped the keycard on his belt to the lock, and it flashed green. He held it open for me and followed close behind with my bag.

"Bath, closet, safe, TV, bed, mini bar," he said, flicking on the lights. "The mini bar's empty, but LiquorQuik on 13th is around the corner and has the best deals." He leaned against the bathroom door frame, idly switching the light on and off.

"You know all the hot spots, don't you?" I expected he was hanging around, hoping for a tip, but the smallest bill I had was a twenty. I pulled one from my wallet and offered it, folded in quarters between my first and middle fingers. "Thank you."

He stared at my bill for a long breath, biting his thumb. Then, without raising his chin, he snatched it, looking up at me through his lashes.

"You look like a tequila boy," he said, spinning to the hall. He was gone through the door to the stairs before I processed what he'd said enough to question what he meant by it. The last I saw of Raul was a perfect ass in white cotton. I'd been so captivated by his chest and arms, his dark eyes and hair, that I hadn't yet noticed how his ass might have been poured into those pants.

The phone rang in my room, and I let the door slowly close to answer it.

"Hello, Mister Lopez; this is Martina at the front desk. I wanted to make sure you got to your room and ask if there was anything you needed."

I'd barely been in my room for five minutes... "Thanks, yes, I'm fine. Maybe a wake-up call for six?"

"Certainly, sir. There will be coffee and complimentary breakfast in the lobby." She hung up without giving me a chance to respond.

Weird... But I saw how she eyed Raul. I imagined her in the lobby, calling to check up on her employee, then hanging up on me as he strolled through the lobby, whistling with my Jackson in his tight pocket.

Six would be here before I knew it, so I went through my usual hotel ritual. I turned the air down as far as it would go, stripped to my trunks, and headed into the bathroom with my toiletry bag. The shower called to me, begging me to rinse off the collective breath of the other hundred and twenty people I'd shared air with at thirty thousand feet.

"You look like a tequila boy," I repeated Raul's words and snorted into the water running down my face. What in all the hell did that mean? I imagined opening my hotel door to him, leaning against the frame, and holding up a plastic bag from LiquorQuik, mini shot bottles tinkling. In my mind, he undid another button of that tight linen shirt and fingered the next.

And I was hard.

I didn't notice stroking myself, as lost in lustful thought as I was, but there I was, leaning against the cold tile, working myself base to tip.

Why not finish off? It'll only help me sleep. I wouldn't take long.

With the steamy water beating down on me, my pace and intent increased. I imagined Raul on his knees in front of me, stroking himself, mouth open and tongue out, ready to take my load. Oh fuck, it really wouldn't—

Two loud bangs on the door.

I froze, and my self-inflicted arousal beat a retreat. Some primal sense in the back of my brain buzzed, warning me whoever knocked was still there, a half dozen feet away through the door. I cut off the tap, grabbed a fluffy white towel, and dripped water to peer out the peephole.

Raul leaned against the wall opposite my door, one foot kicked up beside the other knee, one hand running through his dark hair.

"Just a minute," I said, fleeing farther into my room. My clothes were scattered where I'd tossed them.

You know what? No, fuck it.

I opened the door, holding the towel closed at my hip.

"Hi again," I said, trying to sound casual as if I hadn't just been fantasizing about cumming on this man's tanned face.

Raul bit his lower lip, suppressing a grin, while his eyes ran over me, taking their time around the towel. "Was I right about tequila, señor?" He waggled a cheap liquor pint bottle in his hand, a small plastic shopping bag hanging from his wrist.

He'd undone the fourth button.

"I can't remember the last good decision I made after tequila," I said and leaned against the door.

He kicked off the wall, stopping less than a foot from me, hips swaying with his unheard beat. He seemed taller than before, wider, as he smiled wickedly down at me. "Those are the best kind." Raul offered the bottle between us, but his eyes flicked to the room beyond my shoulder.

The implication was obvious but didn't make sense. A ridiculously hot Latino in tight white pants wanted an invite into my room to drink tequila with him. And to what end? I had to be up in under seven hours. If I screwed up this merger, I'd get fired and could easily sink the company. It could—

"One drink?" I asked, cursing myself as I heard the words cross my lips.

He winked and slipped past me, sliding his hand low across my stomach as he went.

Gulping, I let the door ease closed and followed him toward the bed. Luckily before he reached it, he diverted to get two individually wrapped plastic cups from beside the coffee maker. He dumped ice from the bag around his wrist into a third glass and dropped a cube in with the booze.

"Sorry, I was in the shower," I said, completely unnecessarily, hair still dripping. "Let me get dressed."

"Don't worry about that, señor." Raul moved to within a foot again and offered me a cup half filled with tequila.

Technically, even that much was only one drink...

I tapped my plastic to his and took a tiny sip, trying my best not to visibly shiver and cough. I'd had worse, but not much.

Raul knocked back half his drink and was swaying again to some tune I'd love to hear. With a hand flat on my chest, he pushed me back a step. My knees hit the edge of the bed, and I tripped onto it, focusing on not spilling my drink or letting go of the towel as I did.

His lips parted, his eyes heavy, his gaze swept over me again. His feet moved with his rhythm, one hand pushing through his hair to his neck. Fingers splayed across his collarbone until one caught on his necklace's chain. He brought it to bite between his teeth.

There was no point in adjusting myself by how I tented the towel. The trick would be not cumming just watching the show.

Raul popped another button, pushing the linen aside to pinch a nipple. He tossed the rest of his tequila, flung the plastic cup over his shoulder, then, in one go, unbuckled and ripped his white leather belt free.

I tried another drink, but the cup only made it halfway to my mouth.

He lashed out the belt, catching it around my neck and he dropped onto my lap, knees hugging my hips. The towel's tuck came free, but all his weight was on me, on my hips, on my cock thrusting up at him while he continued moving with his solo dance.

"You probably have to get up early, yeah, señor?" he asked against my ear, his warm breath sending a shiver to my gut.

Yes, I very much did, but I wasn't about to remind him of that while his tight pants pressed against the towel.

He reached steady fingers into my glass, snaring the ice cube. I watched his tongue trace over it, it slide across his full lips, jaw, leaving a water and tequila trail across his clavicle to his nipple. He shifted closer, ran a hand through my hair, and I took the bait, licking up the trail as high as I could, to almost his neck. Fuck, the taste. Tequila, floral bodywash, and clean musk.

Raul slipped his fingers around mine, lifting the glass of tequila to his lips, then leaned the few inches to press those lips to mine. I parted to let his tongue enter, bringing with it the burn of alcohol and a hint of mint from his gum. He ground against me, swaying with the music in his head, both hands clutching his belt to keep me from getting away.

Not that I was going anywhere.

With my hands cupping his ass and my tongue playing against his, I didn't notice the friction growing exponentially until it was too late. I tried to bear down, to clench and stop myself, but, no, this was happening.

Raul felt it beneath him or in my breath and pressed harder against me, slowing his grind while I emptied myself into the towel.

My cock was still pulsing as he pushed back a second later, a hand on my chest, grinning, leaving me with my jaw hanging slack and a hot mess on my hip. He slid backward to plant his feet on the floor, but kept his face, those kissable lips, close. My towel moved with him, snagged against his tight pants, and I snatched the corner of it out of reflex to keep myself covered.

"Time for bed, or do you have a few minutes?" he whispered, his breath laced with tequila.

What did he have in mind? My eyes flicked to the alarm clock on the bedside table. I didn't have time to hit the club with Raul, but... I swallowed hard and nodded. I know the question wasn't binary, but speech eluded me.

Raul extended a hand, palm up, as if inviting me to join him in a dance. My fingers slid across his, and he yanked me up against him, chest to chest. My other hand caught the towel before it dropped away, dangling it between us. He didn't seem to care about me smearing the cum on my hip against his tight white pants. My cock stabbed between us, still as hard as ever, and I felt his straining to be free.

His hands moved across my shoulders, down my arms, then seized at my ribs and spun me away. He kissed my neck while he worked between us, freeing his cock to press hard between my legs. I squeezed him there, shifting to relish the feel of him hard against me.

One hand laid flat on my hip, and the other pressed at the base of my skull, urging me to bend forward.

I obliged, dropping the cum-stained towel to lean with my ass popped out for Raul.

Fucking hell. I came here for financial auditing, not—

A finger, moistened with spit and Raul's pre-cum, slid across my hole and pressed in, homing in on that spot that made me buckle forward with a gasp.

He held me in place, working that one finger for only a moment before the other hand came off my hip to align his cock.

I reached between my legs, past my cock still as hard as ever. Fuck, how I wanted to see him, to taste him, but settled for feeling his girth as he breached me. I wasn't expecting the texture of the condom but I wasn't going to worry about when he had time to get that on. His cock effortlessly found the same spot his finger had, blasting away the tension of his quick entry with a white-hot heat racing up my spine with each slap of his hips against my ass.

"Cum for me," he grunted. "Let me feel it."

The power behind each thrust, the sound of skin slapping, the precision of his strikes, the sensation of my cock smacking against the duvet... But it was his command that sent me over the edge for a second time in minutes.

I painted the bed with more seed than I thought I had left in me. At my first pulse, Raul held tight, and I felt his climax surge deep in me.

My forehead hit the bed, and I had just enough mindfulness to avoid the cum. I'd have to leave an extra tip for house cleaning.

Raul slid free of me, followed by the sound of a zipper. He leaned over me, kissing my shoulder.

"Sleep well, señor," he whispered.

I turned my head in time to see the door closed behind his firm ass.

I lie there, knowing I should get up to shower again or at least wipe off my hip, dick, and ass and get under the covers. Instead, I woke with the wake up call at six and had to rush to get to the office on time. I didn't see Raul on the way out or when I returned to the Ace twelve hours later.

Sitting on the edge of my bed, clean with a fresh duvet, I stared at the half-empty bottle of tequila. My cock twitched. If I ordered room service, would Raul deliver it? Or was he cleaning the rooftop pool in a tiny striped Speedo with his linen shirt open to the evening breeze? Maybe I could find him on one of the apps. Maybe his balls were slapping against another patron's ass at that exact moment.

Shit, that patron was lucky.

I paused with the bedside phone in my hand, stopping myself from ordering a grilled cheese just to see if the guy who delivered it would fuck me.

Fuck it. I stabbed the button, room service menu in hand.

Lucky Me

WE'D KNOWN EACH OTHER for years and finally got to meet in person. Brice and I recognized each other across the train station lobby from avatar photos, hugged, and I got a strong vibe that a kiss might be okay as I studied the gold flecks at the edge of his irises behind his glasses, but that was broken just as quickly as he bent for his luggage.

I realized on the drive home that we never discussed why Brice would take the train from Vancouver. Was "I just wanted to meet you in person" enough of a reason? We'd been talking for a year about meeting in person, but never what we'd do after that. Would we play our game beside each other rather than two thousand miles apart? We could share a single voice chat for the raids. Everyone in our guild already thought we were in a relationship, and heck, our characters were married in the game. We'd been flirting for years, but I never could tell if it was real for Brice.

It was for me.

I guess my goal for his visit would be to tell him how I felt.

We neared my house after twenty minutes of awkward silence on the drive from the station. Street lamps flashed through the windows as I pulled into my neighborhood. Brice's eyes were closed in the passenger seat.

I patted his thigh twice and squeezed. "Any plans on what you want to do tomorrow?" I asked, putting my hands back to ten and two.

"What's fun around here?" he asked. He sounded drowsy, but oh, to hear his deep, smooth voice unfiltered through the mic...

"How about the cider mill?"

"Sure." He yawned. "Sorry, I've been on a train for almost a full day."

"I've got your room all set up with everything you'll need. I'll make us breakfast in the morn-ing, then we go stand in line to shoo away bees for a few hours."

"You're really selling this, babes."

My heart leaped as he brought a bit of our online flirting into the car. I would have grabbed his leg again, but I needed my hands to turn into the garage. That, and he was stuck at my house for three nights, so far from home. If I'd been reading him wrong this whole time and made the first move, a move he didn't want made, I'd ruin the weekend, ruin the best relationship in my life, and leave him in a terrible place. Just like I'd thought of everything he'd need for a comfortable stay, I thought of and overthought everything that could go right and wrong this weekend.

No. Brice would have to make the first move.

Ten minutes later, Brice was opening his luggage on the rack in his room while I stood in the doorway. "Your bathroom's there. My room's just down the hall," I said.

"Thanks. I'll come get you if I need anything." Brice rubbed an eye but smirked. He was exhausted.

"Night," I said, pushing from the doorframe.

"Night, babes," he said with a grin, pursing his lips at me.

We did that every night in-game, thinking nothing of how it would translate to meeting in person. Now, it just left me confused. I wanted to close the distance between us and do what our characters had been emoting for years. Kissing, touching hands, stripping down to small clothes, and finding a secluded spot to fish. Maybe not the fishing part.

I blew the kiss back and rushed away down the hall. I passed the guest bath I'd stocked with travel sizes of anything Brice might have forgotten: toothpaste and brush, deodorant, shampoos, and body washes. In my room, I shut the door behind me in my ensuite, puffing out a breath. He had to feel the same way as me, yeah? Dammit, what if we went the weekend, both waiting for the other to make themself obvious, so neither of us did? That would suck.

I lost myself in my nightly routine: brushing my teeth, washing my face, and cleaning my nightguard. When I returned to my bedroom, Brice was just clicking off his bathroom light and rounding the hallway into the guest room, leaving the door open.

I'd make a move tomorrow. It was supposed to be cold, so I'd stand close while we were waiting for donuts. Maybe I'd put my arm around him on the hayride. If we stayed late enough, the cider mill had haunted attractions. I could startle into him. I was co-president of my high school drama club. I could act when needed.

Lost in thought as I was, I didn't notice I'd been stripping for bed until my trunks were around my knees. I probably shouldn't sleep naked with a house guest, as good of a conversation starter as that might be.

Brice's light was still on.

Shit. I didn't leave him a bottle of water on the nightstand. How terrible of a host could I be?

I hiked up my trunks and jogged down the hall.

"Hey, sorry, do you want a water?" I asked at this doorway.

Brice looked up from where he was pawing through his luggage, still wearing his jeans and hoodie. He started and bit back a grin. I was in such a rush to be a good host that I didn't pay attention to the fact that I was in my small clothes.

"Sure," he said, keeping his eyes trained on mine.

I bolted away downstairs to the garage fridge for a water. Did that count as me making the first move? I nearly expose myself to him. I considered rushing through my room to pull on a pair of sweatpants, but no, that would only raise more questions.

Back upstairs, I almost dropped the water when I stepped into Brice's doorframe. He stood where I'd left him but stripped to boxers printed with four-leaf clovers. Based on the hug at the train station, I expected his broad shoulders and the bit of extra padding around his middle. He turned to me, and I followed the dark, nearly black hair dusting his chest, over his belly, to a trail leading under his boxers. "LUCKY YOU" was printed down the seam of the fly.

Lucky me, indeed.

The text shifted with what lay beneath it. Or maybe it was my imagination.

"I forgot to pack pajamas," he said, and I snapped to lock onto his eyes, swallowing hard.

"That's—" My voice broke, and I cleared my throat. "You can borrow sweats if you want or wear whatever. Or not."

"Thanks." Brice stepped forward to take the water bottle from my hand, his fingers glancing against mine as he did. "I sleep naked at home, but it felt weird to at a stranger's house. I mean, no, not a stranger. We're basically married in a way, but— fuck, you know what I mean."

I did. And he was still close enough to touch.

I had to get out. This wasn't part of the plan.

Muttering another goodnight, I rushed back to my room with my trunks tented and a wet spot forming at the peak.

I had a plan. We'd go to the cider mill, where I'd put the slow burn moves on Brice, gauging his response with each gradual advancement. By this time tomorrow, I'd have a pretty clear bead on if my feelings were reciprocated.

And if they weren't?

I didn't want to think about that.

Why wait? I could resolve this by walking down the hall. Tell Brice how all my flirting had started out playful but morphed into something real over months. Tell him how that first embrace at the train station sparked something deep in my heart that I always knew was there. That I loved him.

His light clicked off.

No, stick to the plan.

Pulling the sheets to my throat, it hit me. Getting Brice his water took less than thirty seconds. He'd rushed to rip off his clothes to match what he'd seen me wearing. He wanted me to see him like that. The idea somehow made my cock even harder, nearly to the point of pain. Maybe I should slip into my bathroom and beat off?

A shadow darkened my doorway, backlit by the weak nightlight in the hall. Brice said nothing as he padded around the bed, pulling back the sheets to slip in beside me.

"What are you—" I started, but he cut me off with a kiss. It was just a light hold of our lips, but it sent an electric thrill down my spine.

"I'm sorry," he said, his breath warm on my lips. "I had to try; had to show you how I feel. If you don't..." He trailed off, maybe not wanting to give voice to the same worries I had.

What could I say? That this was precisely what I wanted? That he jumped to what I'd try to lead toward with gentle nudging over donuts and cider?

I brushed a hand against his cheek and leaned to kiss him back, but he took my fingers in his, kissed my palm, and rolled away, shifting to press his back to my bare chest, shoving his hips, his ass, to my already aching erection. He nestled in, grinding himself against me to be as close as possible, and pulled my hand across his chest so I couldn't get away.

"This feels nice," he sighed.

Not trusting my voice, I instead kissed the back of his neck and squeezed him in a one-armed embrace.

What was this? Just snuggling in our underwear? I flexed my cock, tight against this ass, and he pushed his hips back just a fraction of an inch in response.

I kissed him again, and he kissed my fingers. He released my hand to trace fingertips along my forearm, and I pushed my left arm, which had been awkwardly trapped between us, under his neck and around his chest. My right hand stroked through his chest hair, across the peak of a nipple. Brice shivered in my hold as I went down his ribs. I held him tighter, breathing in the scent of his neck, his hair, kissing his ear. My touch continued down his side to his hip... his thigh...

Fuck! He was naked!

Brice must have sensed what I finally realized and laced his fingers in mine, pulling my hand low across his belly. His hips shifted again, pressing back against me, then forward to brush his cock against my wrist.

I could have cum from that alone.

Leaving my hand on his stomach, he reached back for my hip, picking at the spandex fabric of my trunks. Yes, I'd take those off, but first...

My hand dipped to his cock, holding the base of his girth between my thumb and forefinger, the others cupping his balls. I tested the weight of his cock quickly, giving it a squeeze, then shifted to bridge my hips and pull off my trunks without taking my other arm from under him. Settling back with my dick nestled in the cleft of his ass, my arm slipped low across his belly again for another squeeze.

I'd lusted and pined for this man through text and voice chat for years, vanquished innumerable threats to the realm beside him, and caught fish in our underwear until we were deleting them from our inventories, not wanting to go back to town to vendor them. Now, I held him in my bed, and it was impossible to be closer.

Yet...

Brice slid his hand between our hips, stroked my cock once, twice, five times, and pushed it down to leak precum against his hole. His intent was clear, but I still wanted him to say it.

I took his cock again, stroking his full length in a firm grip, and he arched his back with a soft moan.

"I want to make love to you, Brice," I said between laying kisses across his neck. My cock was already grinding against him, making his ass slick.

"Do it, babes," he said, gasping when my head breached him.

I stayed there, wanting to draw out this first time, knowing a first only happened once, doubting I'd last long after so much build-up. Then, I pressed forward. Each gentle thrust gave him another portion of an inch. I worked his cock with the same rhythm, slow and careful, until I had nothing more to offer, and I held there, flexing in place, stretching him. Not that I had a great deal of experience from either end of this, but it had never been this easy; our shared excitement was so great that the flow of precum was enough.

Each thrust brought more confidence, more force, more moans and gasps from Brice's lips and throat. I wouldn't last much longer. I tried to think of something else, to keep myself on that edge while he moaned in my embrace, sweat prickling my back and legs in the bedroom's chill. We could shift, go from another angle, give me a breath to pull back, but—

"I need to feel you cum in me."

That was the straw that sent me over the edge. Two more thrusts and that familiar seize gripped my balls. Brice clapped a hand against my ass, holding me tight as my cock pulsed, shooting deep into him.

"Fuck!" he squeaked. His ass tightened around me, and he shot over my hand, his belly, and the sheets.

I offered him a few more slow thrusts, hoping I was hitting his prostate, as we caught our breath, trying to come down.

As my aftershocks lessened, I whispered, "Deep breath," and he exhaled as I slid from him.

"I thought you were tired," I said, bringing my hand to my mouth to lick his cum from it.

Brice rolled to his back, heedless of the mess on the sheets, grinning up at me in the dim light. "I found my fourth wind. I wasn't going to sleep until that was settled."

"Well, now we need a shower," I said, pushing up to sit, running my hand through the cum on his belly, bringing it to my lips again. "And I guess we're sleeping in your bed tonight."

I reached behind me for the nightstand lamp, blinking away the momentary dazzle before looking down at Brice. When I'd walked in on him, I tried so hard to keep my eyes pointed where they should, even though I largely failed.

He was far from having a shirtless scene in a Marvel movie, but he was so perfect to me.

He grinned and quickly sat up to kiss me again. "I guess it's good we only talked in the game, not moving to text until I started planning this trip."

"Why's that?"

"Because I'm sure I would have accidentally—" he used air quotes, "—sent you a nude."

I wasn't sure where he was going, but I played along. "And I'd probably accidentally send one back." More air quotes.

"This is better," he said, letting his eyes run over me. "Saving some mystery for our first time."

"I've been dreading this," I mumbled and quickly continued my thought. "I've wanted you, this, us, but didn't know how to make it happen."

"Well, it's happened."

"What should we do for our second time?" I kissed the tip of his nose.

He chuckled. "I don't know about you splitting me with that hog all weekend, or the train ride home will suck."

I snorted, looking down at my dick. That was a severe exaggeration, but I appreciated the sentiment.

Dragging him into my ensuite's wetroom, we showered together, intending to be quick to get to bed. But we started making out, and I dropped to my knees, swallowing every drop of Brice. He wanted to reciprocate, but I told him it would have to wait, reminding him he was tired and things would be better after a good night's sleep.

While drying off, I tried not to think ahead to the end of the weekend, when we'd make that trip back to the train station. Instead, I focused on what would fill the moments between. Every one of those hours, every minute, every second, would be with Brice at my side. All the time knowing what we wanted: each other.

Lucky me.

Cap'n Hank

THIS WAS ONLY OUR fourth time seeing each other, Henry and I.

We first met in passing through mutual friends. I was arriving at our friend's place as he was leaving. There were plenty of prolonged glances, but we never exchanged more than a hello as he rushed out the door. Then he blew up my friend's phone all night asking about me. He was shorter than most guys I dated, but damn cute. I asked as many questions about him, but my friend was annoyingly coy with his answers. I got the feeling he didn't want Henry and I to end up together.

I should clarify by saying that my friend was Henry's friend's boyfriend. Those two had a weird relationship. The boyfriends, not one of them and Henry, I mean. The next time I was over to go out, Henry and I went out separately with one of the boyfriends, but came back and slept together. But like, literally slept together, sharing the guest bed. Both shy, both incredibly drunk, I wanted to strip to my boxers as I would at home, but he kept his shirt, and so I did as well. I don't think I slept a wink that night with the heat of his shoulder pressed against mine in the little full bed.

Henry and I started texting after that. It was nothing of any importance, mostly sharing memes and vaguely flirty innuendos. When he invited me to his place for dinner, I decided it would be a date. I lived twenty minutes from Detroit, and he was a half hour past the Ambassador Bridge, so as long as traffic into Canada wasn't bad, he was only an hour away. If we were to continue to date, it wouldn't be the best, but far from the worst. I dressed up nice, tried something new with my hair, and got on the road.

Did I mention my shyness? Neurotic, perhaps clinical shyness? It takes an act of Congress for me to make a move, so it was a real thing for me to make the executive decision that this would be a date.

Either he was just as bad, or I wasn't properly giving off date vibes. We ate Chinese takeout, he put on a movie—some action flick—and I sat down beside him. He got up to make popcorn and sat a little farther away. I concluded it wasn't a date, just hanging out. When I said I should get going, that it was an hour's drive home, his eyes implied he wanted me to stay, either for the night or at least a bit longer, but he saw me to the door, hugged me, and asked me to text him when I got home safely. He said the last bit while focusing on my lips. I wanted to kiss him, but none of his actions that night made me think he wanted that.

After an uneventful drive, I texted him as promised, and his reply came almost instantly.

me: Just pulled in! Thank you for dinner. I had a nice time.

Henry: Thank you! I really liked having you over. We should hang out again when I get back.

Back from where? This was awkward. He hadn't mentioned a vacation or work trip. Then, it struck me that I had no idea what he did for a living. All I knew was it was something to do with the big cargo ships that went through the Detroit River and around the Great Lakes.

> me: That would be nice!

> Henry: Ten days! I can't wait to hug you again <3

I ghosted him for two days after that. How dare he. Henry showed no physical interest in me during the four hours I was in his house, and then he says the highlight of the night was the embrace at the very end. I would have kept ignoring him, but I convinced myself I could have done more to express my interest. So, I sent him a BS message about dropping my phone in the toilet and having to leave it off while it sat in rice. We picked up with our memes and lame attempts at flirting like nothing happened.

Finally, I grew a pair and got to the point.

> me: Hey, could I bring a bag when I come over? That's a long drive to make late at night.

> Henry: You read my mind! I wanted you to stay last time. I couldn't get up the nerve to ask.

> me: I couldn't get up the nerve to ask to stay. Aren't we a pair? :)

On the seventh day, he asked if I could meet him the following evening and gave me an address somewhere scary in Detroit. It wasn't just my dick accepting the invite. Henry and I were building up a nice rapport with a lot in common: cycling, comic books, big dogs.

I triple checked my GPS as I pulled into the dark parking lot and around the warehouse to a view of the river and the massive cargo ship filling it.

> Henry: Tell Jill you're there to see me, and she'll drive you over.

The only other sign of life was a pickup truck, so I parked by it. A hardened woman wearing warm flannel was propped up in the truck's bed, reading a book. She tensed when I approached, and her hand went to her hip.

Fucking hell! Not just her hip, but the gun holstered on it!

"Ah, hi?" I said with my palms raised and my overnight duffle bag drooping from my elbow. "I'm here to see Henry. Are you Jill?"

She squinted at me for a breath, then chuckled. "Cap'n Hank. Yeah, said he was expecting someone."

Goddamn, I was slow. That explained why our mutual friends called Henry "Cap'n." I assumed

he just worked on the big ships, but he cap-
tained them. How does one even begin that
career path? I smirked, imagining myself like a
call boy coming to tend to the captain's needs
while docked at port.

"Get in," Jill said, nodding at the two-seater
motorboat at the bottom of slick concrete stairs
leading into the water. She radioed ahead, and
by the time I was climbing the narrow metal
stairs up the ship's side, Henry was grinning
down at me from the top.

"You made it!" he said. His body language
screamed of anxiety, and he quickly waved us
into a door, out of the interested eyes of the
few others lingering on the desk. It made sense,
wanting to avoid displays of affection around
his crew.

"You didn't tell me you were the captain," I
said as he wove through the ship. I was utterly
lost after a few turns.

"You didn't ask."

"Fair."

I had no basis for comparison, but his quarters seemed nice. They opened first to a small
office stacked with paperwork, all weighed
down with polished rocks. Then, another heavy
door into the living room with a couch and TV.

The bathroom was off that, as was the bed-room.

"I got us dinner from the mess. It's just warmed up lasagna, but it's all—"

Henry interrupted himself by kissing me. He had to stand on his toes to do it, and I didn't re-turn it at first. He pushed himself back a second after I slipped a hand around his stomach.

Wiping a finger across his lips, he smiled shyly up at me. "I've been waiting to do that for weeks now. Let's grab dinner and put the movie in."

Fuck the lasagna! Fuck the movie! More kiss-ing, please!

I could have grabbed and pushed him to the couch, but I let him pass me back through his office.

On the way to the mess hall, Henry diverted our route to show me the cargo hold. I don't know why that would be interesting, but he said they were loading in some concrete component and something about the machinery was inter-esting.

It wasn't, just conveyors and forced air to move stuff to the far end of the hold, but I wasn't going to tell him that.

We were about to leave when I got a blast of something in the face. I was blinded with my eyes stinging before I knew what happened. I felt Henry's hands on me, rushing me somewhere, telling me to tilt my head back, and then freezing cold water pouring over my face. The pain subsided after a minute, and I could see again. When I looked around, I saw a lot of Henry's crew staring at us.

"Let's get you back," he whispered. "I have an eyewash station in my quarters."

He took my wrist, pulling me from the cargo hold and away from the crew's interest.

With the door shut behind us, Henry held my cheeks and peered into each of my eyes. "Are you okay? I don't know what happened there."

"Me either. I'm okay."

"Are you sure? Do you need the eyewash?"

"No," I blinked. "I'll be fine."

"Your shirt's soaked. Want me to hang it up in the bathroom to dry?"

"Trying to get me out of my shirt already?"

He touched a finger to his lips. "Should I take off mine, too?"

"I think you should."

His hands went to the bottom hem, but I closed what little space there was between us, folding my fingers over his to pull his shirt over his head. He did the same for me, and we stood chest to chest in his living room, water dripping from my hair.

"They, ah..." He started and created an inch of space. "If they file a report about what happened... Well... I'm not supposed to have guests while the ship is loading."

I shifted in, taking away his inch. "I won't tell anyone."

He looked up and pressed his lips to mine, gently, tentatively. His hands moved around me, tracing fingertips across my lower back.

"Dinner's a bust, I'm sorry," he said, his breath against mine. "Do you still want to watch the movie? I have popcorn here." His gaze flicked to the couch beside us.

"I was just nearly blinded by construction particulate. I don't know if I could manage through a movie," I said with a smirk.

"I feel bad enough already." He paused to look at the TV across from the couch, then toward the bedroom door. "We can watch it on my laptop, and the bed's more comfortable than the couch."

The couch looked fine, if not old, but I wouldn't argue with his hand in mine, tugging me toward the door.

We stepped out of our shoes to get into bed in our jeans and socks. I tugged off the latter, and he did, too, before reaching for a laptop on his side table.

"What movie do you want..."

I settled along his side with a knee over his, my toes brushing the top of his foot, my head at his shoulder, and a hand over his across his belly. Though I knew it was laughable to most, I internally applauded my forwardness.

"...watch?" he finished and set the laptop on his other side. His hand on his stomach slipped around mine, so my palm was flat against him. Henry tilted his head to me, with our noses an inch apart. Our lips were just a little far-ther. "Hi," he whispered.

"Hi." I shifted to kiss him, tracing my tongue over his lip as I pulled away. "What about a massage?"

"I think I owe you one after getting blasted in the face."

"Maybe it'll lead to that again," I winked

We were both already flushed from the warmth and closeness, but Henry's visibly deepened. He said nothing, but nodded and rolled away from me, to his stomach.

I had no actual knowledge of how to properly perform a massage, but I mounted Henry's backside, my crotch to his ass, determined to do my best. With his face buried in the pillow, I started at his neck, pushing deep through the cords of muscle to his shoulders. When I got to his ribs, I realized precum was starting to soak through my jeans, creating a dark spot visible even in the dim light. Henry moaned and sighed with each push, each stroke, each graze of my fingertips. Lower and lower down his back... I wished he weren't wearing the jeans and belt.

I could have worked my way back up and started again, but Henry glanced over his shoulder, grinning. He shifted under me, and I lifted to my knees to let him roll to his back before I settled on his thighs.

The jeans had to go.

I worked his belt, and he bridged his hips to help me pull off his pants, leaving him in dark green plaid boxers. Henry sucked in a deep breath as my fingertips glided over his chest to his ribs, belly button, then traced the elastic band to his hip bone. I leaned down, leaving kisses in the same path, pausing with his boxer's waistband filling my vision.

"Is this okay?" I whispered, and he replied with a nod through heavy eyes and a barely audible whimper.

I grasped the band, and Henry again lifted his hips for me to pull his boxers down and past his feet.

I started at his knee, leaving the ghosts of kisses along his inner thigh, avoiding his throbbing cock for the moment and across his belly. The pressure in my chest rose, forcing me to move more slowly lest I pop. Back down, a little nearer. His cock brushed my cheek, and he sucked in a sharp breath.

"Are you still okay?" I asked again. He nodded and whimpered again but threaded his fingers through my hair and lifted his hips, pushing his cock against my throat.

Back down, gentle kisses, gentle tracing of my fingertips. Henry moaned, whimpered, and hissed with every touch. Every hint of his pleasure made my cock twitch and ache. I had to slow down even more. Every minute display of his pleasure redoubled in me, bringing me closer to the line. I dragged the tip of my tongue from the base of his sack to the tip of his dick, licking the precum from his crown, and he shivered the whole way. I repeated the gesture three more times. His thighs quaked. My boxers were soaked with precum.

I took him fully to my throat, always moving slowly with minimal pressure.

"Fuck!" He shouted and pounded a fist on the sheets. "Hold on," he gasped, dipping his hips into the mattress to pull out of my mouth. "It's... It's been a while."

"Should I stop?"

"No, I just... need a second." Henry exhaled through pursed lips. "What about you?"

I pushed a hand down my front, giving my cock one good squeeze. It surged at my touch, ready to blow from knowing how I made him feel. "Don't worry about me." I stroked his inner thigh, down the sides of his balls, up the center, and took a firm hold on the base of his dick. He gasped, whimpered, and came, arcing past my hand to splash in his trimmed pubes. I held firm, savoring how he tensed with each convulsion.

Watching him grab a fist full of sheets was enough for me, and though I tried to hold it back, I released into my boxers.

He panted, slowly letting go of the sheets. "What about you?" he asked again between breaths.

I dipped a hand into my pants and held it up to the light to show him my mess.

A phone in the wall over the bed rang, and Henry snatched it before it rang a second time. "Yes?" While he listened intently, I hovered awkwardly over him, one hand coated in my cum and a little of his. "Be right there." He hung up and shifted under me. I slid to the side to let him scoot to the edge of the bed.

Henry looked around for his clothes with one hand scooping cum from his stomach. "I'm needed on the bridge. I won't be long." He found his clothes in record time and gave me a hasty kiss before he left the room.

I sprawled out on the bed, breathing the pillow scented with his shampoo and fantasizing about spending the night with Henry in my arms. After a while, I went to the bathroom and used a washcloth to wipe my eyes again, then tried to clean as much cum out of my boxers as possible. I ended up taking a shower and was back in bed, naked, when Henry returned almost two hours later.

"Sorry, I..." he started, avoiding looking me in the eye. He took a moment to find his words, then told me he was called up to perform some minor position adjustment, which only he was qualified to do. Then his first mate pulled him aside, saying she was made aware of the incident in the cargo hold involving me. He reminded me of the regulation stating there were not supposed to be unauthorized people aboard when loading. "I wanted you to stay the night, but..."

He didn't have to say it. I slipped out of bed, and he averted his gaze from me. I pulled on cum-stained boxers and a still-wet shirt. Before he opened the door out of his quarters, Henry grabbed my elbows for one more kiss. His eyes again wouldn't meet mine as he pulled back, but I wasn't sure if it was sadness or guilt. Or both. How much trouble was he in for having me aboard?

He led me, silently, like leading a prisoner to solitary confinement or the gallows, to the stairs leading down to Jill waiting in the little motorboat.

I got home to a text from him.

> Henry: Sorry about that. I'll call you in a few days.

> me: I had a great time tonight. Wish I could have stayed, but I get it. Looking forward to next time! <3

But, there was no next time. Henry never called or texted after that. When I asked our mutual friends about him, they admitted they still hung out with Henry regularly but otherwise quickly changed the subject. After a month, my eyes were no longer randomly stinging. Another month after that, I was staring at the screen of unanswered texts to him, scrolling back through our clumsy flirting, wondering what would have gone differently that we might still be talking. I still followed him on social media, but I wasn't about to bother him on Instagram if he wouldn't reply to a text. Maybe he got in deep trouble for having me on the ship. Maybe I wasn't his first offense.

Another three months passed, and Henry's feed started to include pics of him with another guy with kind of a goofy face and hair, but a nice smile. All his other photos were of boats or birds, so it stuck out. They were at some party together and were way too close not to be intimate.

Whatever there might have been between us was no more, ended before it started. Maybe we would get back to talking some day, and I'd find out what happened, but I'd have to be content if I never knew. I'd certainly never know if I didn't express some interest outside of our abandoned text thread.

I gave the party photo a like.

Also By Dirk

Other works by Dirk Mourningwood
La Luce's Legacy (2024)
Eros Unzipped (2024)
Eros Unchained (2024)
Eros Unmasked (2025)

About Dirk

 Dirk Mourningwood is an emerging voice in the world of MM erotica, known for his bold storytelling and captivating characters. With a passion for exploring the depths of human desire and the complexities of male relationships, Dirk weaves tales that are both sensual and emotionally resonant. His writing invites readers into a world where passion knows no bounds and love transcends all barriers. When he's not crafting his next tantalizing story, Dirk enjoys immersing himself in period dramas, practicing kenjutsu, and playing disc golf with his lab Rodger.

www.ingramcontent.com/pod-product-compliance
Lightning Source LLC
Chambersburg PA
CBHW051850170626
46807CB00003B/1414